MORTAL FLIP

A Home Renovator Mystery

By: M. E. Bakos

Copyright

Copyright © 2024 by M. E. Bakos
All rights reserved.

No part of this publication may be reproduced, distributed, or transmitted in any form or by any means, including photocopying, recording, or other electronic or mechanical methods, without the prior written permission of the publisher, except as permitted by U.S. copyright law. For permission requests, contact mebakos@yahoo.com

The story, all names, characters, and incidents portrayed in this production are fictitious. No identification with actual persons (living or deceased), places, buildings, and products is intended or should be inferred.
Book Cover by Angi, Pro Ebook covers.
First edition 2024

For information: email mebakos@yahoo.com

Amazon Print ISBN: 979-8-9867889-3-7
Ingram Print: ISBN: 979-8-9867889-1-3

For Joseph Sebesta and Chipper

Praise for the Home Renovator Mystery series:

From Diane Donovan's Killer Flip, Editorial review:
"Fans of amateur sleuths and powerful female investigators will find *Killer Flip*, Book 4 in a Home Renovator mystery series, to be just the ticket for a different, more compelling first-person mystery read." She goes on, "Cozy mystery library collections need to place *Killer Flip* at the top of their acquisition list. It deserves a prominent place and recommendation in such circles whether or not readers have familiarity with Katelyn's prior house renovation and murder-solving adventures.

From Liz Konkel's Editorial Review of Killer Flip for Reader's Favorite:

"M.E. Bakos has a fun writing style with delightful details" She goes on, "Bakos has a style that gives substance to the town through Katelyn's perspective of it such as feeling the eyes of Crocus Heights (the town) watching her. If you love renovation and murder mysteries, Killer Flip is a perfect read"

Chapter 1

Myra Alexandria Payten picked up the keys I had tossed on the counter in my new project, a two-story rehab on Thrush Street in Crocus Heights, a small suburb outside of Minneapolis, Minnesota.

"Engraved initials. Nice. ABC in script on a gunmetal piece." She ran long tapered fingers over the impressions, and gasped, "Oh no! Arthur Brett Cook!"

"Who?" I frowned. A twinge started in my stomach. My name is Katelyn Baxter, Home Rehab Specialist. I started renovating houses because of an unfortunate dismissal from my full-time, insurance-and-benefits-paying employer, and with the encouragement of my BFF, Myra. Home renovation is my happy place, but it has been a ride.

"That is the man who was murdered. He worked at Maxim's." Maxim, or better known as Max, was the biggest employer in town. Anyone who was anyone worked at Max. Workers claimed there were no bad jobs at the corporation, and it was the best employer around.

"He was found dead in a field. It has been in the paper and on the news. They suspect coworkers because he complained to HR that someone was harassing him by dumping cola on his desk and computer." Her gaze narrowed, examining the keys. "He reported his keys went missing on more than one occasion."

"Really?" The twinge I felt earlier morphed to a lump in the pit of my stomach as I faced Myra. "Do you know the names of the coworkers?"

"Sean Young. He was in the IT department." She frowned and added, "They have been investigating everyone in the department, but another man, Nathan Winner, was named in the newscast too."

I groaned, "Sean Young is my home seller."

"Oh, no!" Myra winced; her lips pursed.

"We have to call the police," she said. She dangled the keys in front of my eyes as if to jolt me back to reality. "They will want these if they belong to Arthur Brett Cook."

"Good grief, not another murder!" Resigned, I added, "I'll make the call."

While we waited for the police to arrive, I remembered the burst of enthusiasm we'd had earlier when we toured the home.

"This is a great house!" Myra had exclaimed, gazing at the open concept layout, where a couple could watch children play in the family room while they prepared meals in the kitchen.

The friendly city has a quaint system of naming streets after birds. After flipping houses on Bluebird and Warbler Streets, I Googled the thrush and found that the female is reddish-brown with a mottled brown underbelly. The male has glossy black feathers and is showy with a yellow eye ring around its eye and an orange-yellow bill. Isn't showy the way of the male species?

"It is a terrific place, isn't it?" I mused. "The owner updated the carpeting and painted. I want to change out the fireplace mantel to freshen the look of the family room. There is miscellaneous stuff to get rid of and some deep cleaning, a few odds and ends, but it is a beauty. A little painting, minor fixes, staging, and I'm done."

"You said it was for sale by the owner?"

"Yes. You know my favorite thing to do is to search out new properties to flip, and he had just put out a sign. I stopped, and we talked. He had a very good price, so I jumped on it."

"Why did he want to sell?" Myra looked stylish, as usual. Her hair and nails were freshly done. Her hazel eyes sparkled with hints of green and blue.

"His wife wanted out of the place."

"Okay, tell me more?" She wrinkled her nose and studied me.

"He said that it was his home when they married. She was never comfortable in the place. It was a 'me or the house' situation." My mouth tightened, and I stuffed my free hand into the pocket of my well-worn jean jacket.

"Good for her. A woman needs her own home."

"I'm glad you feel that way." My head down, I pulled out drawers. Myra sensed my evasiveness, and I felt her eyes boring through the back of my head while I dug through a kitchen drawer and tossed odds and ends into a box to sort out later. I pulled out the set of keys with an engraved tag attached and remarked, "Somebody might miss these," and tossed them on the counter.

"How is it going with the sheriff?" she asked.

I considered her innocent query and continued with the next drawer, avoiding her question.

Don Williams, the sheriff of Crocus Heights, was my fiancé. He had popped the question last Christmas Eve, surprising me with a beautiful diamond ring. I was not in the best form. I had contracted some kind of bug and was a mess of cough syrup and any decongestant I could lay my hands on. For all the buildup and anticipation, the evening promised, I pretty much passed out on the sofa at his mansion until nearly midnight but revived long enough for his proposal. It was sweet and thoughtful, and I said yes in a flash, despite our skittish relationship.

"Hum, it's going," I said. My head was down as I picked through the drawers.

"Sean seemed like an okay guy. He worked with computers." I shook my head. "He did have a quick temper. The pen he used to sign the documents dried up. He shook it a few times and got frustrated, then he hurled it at the trash can. I gave him another pen." Shrugging, I said, "I put it down to stress about selling. Otherwise, he was of average height and a slightly pudgy build. Thick brown hair in a buzz cut, brown eyes. He was not a man who stood out in a crowd."

"Except that he was in a hurry to sell?" Myra asked with a slight frown.

"He explained that he and his wife had found a place closer to her work as a teacher. They put a down payment on it but didn't want to carry two mortgages." I stopped and stared at Myra. "But where was I, if this was all over the news?"

"You've been busy." She smirked.

"It's been hectic." Don and I had reveled in our newly engaged status with couples' time filled with movies and dining. I had been deliriously happy until one night he brought me home, settled on the sofa, with Boots, my Tuxedo rescue cat, and said, "It'll be nice when we're all living together in my home," while he stroked Boots' head.

"What makes you think I want to move in with you?" I stopped, stunned. "It's your house, not our home." He sat up and moved Boots aside.

"But it is a lovely place. Plenty of room for both of us and Boots," he offered cautiously.

"Let's not forget the housekeeper," I snipped.

He flushed, "Yes. I like Esther and expect her to stay on. I like my home."

"I like my home, too," I said, crossing my arms, with my head tilted and eyes narrowed.

"Yes, Katelyn. It is comfortable. Quaint." A chuckle slipped out.

"So, it's not a mansion," I said, testy. "It's like a comfortable pair of shoes." My sofa was covered with a bright yellow throw that signaled spring and saved the couch from the wear of the cat's shedding. Bookshelves were filled with books, pictures, and the bric-à-brac of my life - a vase, candles, souvenirs from traveling. His home was grand, with spacious rooms and a spiral staircase to a second floor with several bedrooms, each with private baths.

"I didn't mean it that way." His deep blue eyes dimmed.

"I know how you meant it." My lips pressed together.

And the fight was on. We faced off, both of us firm that a home meant sanctuary, and both of us solidly dug into our present homes. In short, neither of us liked change.

After a few choice words, he slipped on his brown leather bomber jacket and left. "I'll call you." Code for when donkeys fly. That was a week ago, with total silence since then.

Chapter 2

While Myra and I waited on the steps of the rehab, I spotted a stout, middle-aged woman staring from the sidewalk of the residence next door. I groaned inwardly, ducking, as she crossed her lawn to where we stood. This was not a good time to meet the neighbors.

The sheriff's car arrived, and I took a deep breath, bracing myself for Don, hoping against hope that he had stayed in his office shuffling papers, and not gone out on the call. No such luck.

With shoulders squared, he strode to the stoop of the two-story renovation where we lingered.

Upon seeing the sheriff's car, the neighbor hesitated and feigned a detour to study a bush, with a side eye fixed toward us. Don's body blocked the woman's view of Myra and me. When I peered around his broad shoulders, I saw that she had reluctantly retreated to her front door.

"Katelyn." He nodded. His eyes lit up for a moment before he turned to Myra. "It's good to see you. Hope your brother is well."

"He is. I will tell him you asked." Myra's brother was the police chief, a fact that gave her an inside edge on the doings of the small burg. She never divulged who was detained for what, but you knew there had to be some gossip around the town.

"We found a set of keys," I said, holding them by the name tag. "Myra said the engraved initials are the same as a man who worked at Maxim's and who was murdered?"

He grasped the keys and examined them.

"So, you found another place to rehab," he said flatly. "In a week." He shot me a cool glance.

"Yes. I did." I stared at him; my back stiffened. It seemed much longer. But, yep, just a week. I'll concede, we should have discussed my career earlier, but hadn't, reveling in the fog of being newly betrothed.

"You might have put the rehab business on hold while we are engaged? Maybe quit it all together." He was still grumpy.

"It's how I pay my bills. Some people have jobs to pay for their expenses." Yes, I was snarky and stubborn because of our tiff over my home versus his home. He had recently disclosed he was wealthy because he had sold the family auto dealership. And he fessed up only after I confronted him as a result of some online sleuthing with Myra. It rankled that he had not been more forthcoming. His reason for not disclosing earlier was that he didn't want it to be a "thing." The reason I, or any woman, would want to date him. I was irritated that he thought so little of me.

Myra had talked me off the ledge and convinced me it wasn't personal; it was the way some rich people think. People like them because they have money, not for who they are. It made sense in a weird way. If I was loaded, I guess I would be more careful.

"I plan to keep flipping houses," I said, folding my arms across my chest and lifting my chin.

"Huh." He shrugged. "Don't need to."

"It's my passion," I said, standing firm.

"I hope I would be your passion." He tilted his head, his mouth softened, and his gaze held my eyes.

I wavered under the very blue stare of his eyes and stammered, "People can have more than one passion."

"Uh hum." Myra cleared her throat and glanced between the two of us. Sensing impending fireworks, she had drifted toward the kitchen and waited a few feet away by the sink. I kept my focus on Don, and she pretended she hadn't heard our conversation, asking with a bland expression, "What about the keys?"

"I'll take them. We may have to search the house again. They could belong to someone else with the same initials. There is no direct evidence that Sean Young killed Arthur Cook. A couple of news reports avowed they were good friends and coworkers."

"The paper said he was a person of interest because their friendship soured. Arthur got the promotion Sean wanted and thought he should have received," Myra said. "The news said everyone in the department had been questioned, and that another man, Nathan Winner, is under suspicion, too."

"Why?" I asked, my brows shot up.

"He was competing for the same position."

"Okay." That made sense.

I viewed Myra as she went on. "There were others at Maxim's that had run-ins with him. Arthur wasn't very popular."

"Too bad. But the news reported his body was found?" My attention returned to the sheriff.

"Yes." Don said, grimly, "He was found in a cornfield with a gunshot wound to the back of the head."

"That's terrible!" I gasped.

"It is." His mouth pressed into a firm line.

"How soon will you know if the keys belong to Arthur?" Myra asked.

"We will check with his parents and his girlfriend. They should know whether this is his keychain. I'll get back to you."

"Can I continue the rehab?" I asked.

"No. For now, we'll pause the work."

My shoulders fell. Exasperated, I frowned and muttered, "I'll lock up." Gathering my messenger bag, I went to the entry. Avoiding his stare, I could feel that he and Myra exchanged glances behind me.

Lightly gripping my arm on the way out, Don said in a low tone, "Katelyn, we need to talk." Shrugging, I threw up my hands and went outside, where Myra joined me. Exasperated, he left us standing on the stoop watching while he firmly trekked to his car, got in, slammed the door, and drove off.

"So, there appears to be an issue between you two?" Myra asked. She brushed back a stray hair from the sudden gust of wind in the early spring day and faced me.

"Not only did he just shut down my rehab, but . . .?" I sputtered. "He wants me to give up my passion to live in his big house."

"Does the housekeeper come with?" Myra bantered.

"Not the point. But yes."

"Marriage means sacrifices. If it means giving up crawling around in houses with dead body mysteries and living in a mansion with a housekeeper?" She shrugged and grinned. Her eyes twinkled. "You do what you have to do."

I snickered, catching her humor, then dissolved into laughter.

"Yeah. I guess that's pretty bad. But I love the challenge of a new project, fixing it up for someone to love, making it whole again." It was like repairing my chaotic life. I wiped tears of mirth from my eyes. "Don looked very handsome, didn't he?" I had played it cool while he was near, but I missed him. "He said he wants to be my passion."

"Yes. And he should be." Myra nodded and smiled.

"I do not want to give up what I do, or my home. What do I do?" I wailed. I had let myself be swept away with the romance of being engaged, wooed, and comforted by someone who wanted to have a future, without thinking through the reality of life with another man.

"Life is a journey," she said, and gave me her best Mona Lisa smile.

Chapter 3

"Go ahead with the rehab." Don called the next morning. He was brisk.

"That was fast." I was pleased, but curious about the quick work.

"The keys don't belong to the dead man. We checked his condo and car. No match. I'll have my deputy drop them by. They could be spares for the rehab?"

"Hum, that's possible. I didn't try them." I may have been too quick to presume they belonged to the dead man. Myra's news about the connection between my seller and Arthur Brett Cook had negated the possibility they were extra keys. It was not the first time I had jumped to the wrong conclusion.

I hung up. At least we were talking. That made me smile. I putzed around, getting ready for work. I had asked Wayne Hamer, my neighbor and handyman, to check out the project. Most of the rehab I could handle. The owner had done a good job of updating. I had jumped at the place partly because Wayne was a newlywed and had enough adjustments to make with a wife who sleepwalks. But I wanted him to redo the fireplace mantel. It needed to be refreshed. He was a semi-retired carpenter and an expert with wood. He would have some advice about updating it.

My mind was still on Don. He needed to explain himself and his ridiculous assumptions about marriage and women. This was the twenty-first century, after all. If he wanted to talk about us, it was his move.

I removed the huge diamond engagement ring from my finger, placing it on my bedside nightstand, and muttered "Can't rehab a house wearing that gem, anyway." Giving the ring a wistful look, I finished dressing, and left for work.

With my mug filled with strong java, I wondered where the heck Wayne Hamer was. By 8:00 a.m. Wayne usually rapped at my door, ready for work and wanting a "to go" cup of my Colombian brew. He lived down the hall with Gillie, his new bride.

There were four units in the Tudor style townhome where I lived. Currently, just two of the four units were occupied. He and Gillie lived together, but each had kept their original units, deciding they would take their time merging their lives after living as single adults. My unit was the first, with Gillie's vacant unit next, then the Hamer's new residence, and Wayne's old place at the end. I decided against knocking on their door. It was eerily quiet as I left the building and headed over to the new rehab.

I fumed all the way to the new job, my mind replaying the issues between Don and me. He had presumed, no assumed, I would move into his mansion. There had been no talk of a "we" home; it was his home. It was a gorgeous place. But his, down to the dishes, the carpet, the drapes, and everything else. It would be a monstrous redo, but he seemed resistant to change. Once, I had made an offhand comment about the lack of color in the immense kitchen. He had sniffed and said, "It looks clean."

"White it is, then." I shrugged, did an eye roll, and dropped the subject.

The house on Thrush Street reminded me of how stark the interior or exterior of a bachelor home could be. Sean's wife had added no feminine touches to the outside, and there were no signs of spring flowers, no bushes, just grass. The inside was basic beige, with all personal traces removed. Perfect for my quick once over and sale. At least Don had landscaped the grounds, and his house had a more welcoming façade than the one on Thrush Street. The masculine furnishings were comfortable, too.

A cruiser pulled up and parked beside me in the driveway of the new rehab. I looked over to a female officer who stepped from the squad car and waited while I hopped out of my Ford.

"Are you Katelyn Baxter?"

"Yes." I looked at the blonde stocky officer, her hair pulled back and shoulders squared. Her most compelling features were close-set, bright blue eyes that focused on me with a stare.

"Sheriff Williams wanted me to return these to you." She held out the set of keys I had given him the day earlier.

"Great. Thank you." I palmed the keys.

"No problem." She gave a curt nod and got back inside the squad car.

My shoulders tensed from her abrupt manner, and I stiffly marched to the rehab. With a shrug, I tried the set of keys in the lock. The key turned easily, and I frowned, surprised. They were spares. So, why were they tagged ABC? What was up with that?

"Hello there?" A woman's voice called from the lawn separating the two homes. She wheezed as she walked. I paused while unlocking the front door and turned to greet the short female, who carried a flyer. It was the neighbor whom I had seen the day before while Myra and I lingered on the steps, waiting for the sheriff.

"This belongs to the resident here," she held out a weekly grocery shopper.

I blinked and took the proffered paper. It was a local shopper delivered free to residents in the area.

"I got two this week, so this one must be yours," she smiled expectantly. She had short brown hair and a booming voice. I had seen her work in her front garden in a well-kept white rambler and observed her covert gaze at the police presence at the rehab.

"Thank you." I smiled in return, bemused. It didn't seem worthwhile to bring over the advertisement, but I would be polite. My phone rang while the door was partially open. I entered and was about to close the door. "Katelyn Baxter, pleased to meet you." I nodded goodbye to the neighbor while glancing at the display. "I have to take this."

"By the way, my name is Dorothy, Dorothy Barker. People call me Dottie. So, I saw the police here?" She nodded, her eager expression fading as I closed the door.

"What's up, Wayne?" I tossed the spare keys into my messenger bag.

"Kiddo, I got a problem." Wayne called me "Kiddo," his nickname, hardly ever by my given name. I liked it. It made me feel younger than my thirty-five years. Although, I only admit to twenty-eight. Age is just a number, right?

"What problem?" I asked.

"I can't work today. Gillie is in jail."

"What? What do you mean?"

"That new deputy, Morgan Clark, picked her up while she was sleepwalking and took her in. Clark says Gillie confessed to killing Walter and claimed she poisoned him."

"Walter Gilman, her first husband? That doesn't make any sense. She wouldn't kill anyone!"

"They got it on tape. They have to check it out. I know she didn't. She couldn't. She doesn't have a mean bone in her body. Murder? That is a crock." He sounded worried, even as he declared Gillie's innocence.

"Take all the time you need," I said, and then asked, "She was sleepwalking again?"

"Yep."

"She was having a nightmare," I suggested.

"I think so, too, but now they have to investigate." He snorted.

"Don't worry about the job here. Just work it out with Gillie." After hanging up from Wayne, shaking my head at the absurd idea of Gillie killing anyone, I laid a tarp around the base of the fireplace and took a crowbar to the mantel. After a few well-placed lifts, the top board gave way. Out fell a small revolver, clattering to the floor.

"Dang it!" I knelt to inspect the handgun.

"Great, a gun." I heaved a sigh while staring at the weapon, and muttered, "Arthur Cook was shot."

I knew enough after flipping a few houses not to touch a possible murder weapon and called Don. "You need to come by the Thrush Street rehab."

"You're ready to talk?" He asked in a low tone. "About living in my home?"

"No." My stomach gave a flutter. "I found a gun."

He let out a deep sigh, then asked, "Where?"

"It fell out when the mantel was removed."

"I'll be right there."

The dial tone sounded before I could say goodbye or protest it wasn't my fault there was a gun in my rehab.

While I waited, I released the breath caught in my throat and continued inspecting the weapon. I knew little about guns, but as they went, this firearm was nice looking. It had a black barrel with a brown base with a smooth, rounded grip, and looked like a weapon that could be handled with relative ease. If I wanted to shoot anything. With a shudder, I decided not so much.

Don rapped, and I opened the door to the frustrated officer of the law. His nose twitched and his mouth was tight.

"You found a gun." He was businesslike.

"It's on the floor. I didn't touch it." I waved him toward the family room and stepped aside. He brushed past me, his proximity catching me off guard. His intensity was electrifying, and I inhaled while I followed him down the short hall and turned right into the family room. He squatted and examined the gun.

"Three fifty-seven Smith and Wesson revolver," he said, his mouth tightened.

"You said Arthur Brett Cook had been shot?" I asked.

"Yep. I'll bag it. I am stopping work in this rehab. We need to search the place again. Be more thorough."

"Okay." I gulped. "But you don't know if Sean hid the gun. For that matter, you don't know if the weapon belongs to him. It could have been here before he owned the house?"

"That's all true, but it doesn't look good."

"How long will another search take?"

"Not sure."

That was the answer I expected. Noncommittal.

"Do what you have to do." The sight of a gun hidden away made me queasy about this flip. Sean had seemed like any other average seller during the transaction, but in the space of a few days, it appeared there was more to him than the ordinary homeowner. I waited, my arms crossed, while Don bagged the weapon and rose to face me.

"When can we talk, Katelyn?" His gaze softened, and I melted while his eyes traveled my face and down to my hands. He frowned and lifted my left hand, and asked, "No ring?" I stiffened. "I suppose you can't wear it while working on a flip," he groused, and let my hand drop.

"No. It's too beautiful, and I would not want to damage it." I met his gaze.

"You're right." He surveyed me coolly, his mouth puckered. "I guess you're going to keep flipping houses."

"Yes." I stood straight. My face colored under his questioning and the warmth of his touch.

"We will talk more. I have to get back to the station. Be careful, Katelyn. If this is Sean's gun and he killed the man, there is no telling what he would do if he knew you found the weapon."

"I don't think he's dangerous. He seems like a regular guy," I said, thinking back to our interactions. "He was earnest about selling this place, so he would have one less mortgage and live in harmony with his wife."

"What do you mean?"

"His wife didn't like the place. They bought one closer to her teaching job. It was his house, not theirs."

"Sounds familiar." He gave a wry grin.

"It does." I nodded and looked away, the atmosphere tense, then changed the subject. "Wayne said Gillie is being held for killing her first husband. She was sleepwalking, and an officer picked her up."

He relaxed. "I know Wayne and Gillie are your friends, but I can't discuss an ongoing investigation."

"You know Gillie. She was dreaming or something. She would not hurt a fly."

"Uh, huh. I know Gillie, but the officer must check out her statements."

"But if she wasn't awake, how can anything she said be considered true?" I was aghast.

"If she confessed to a crime, they have to investigate," he said.

"After they do their silly inquiry, she'll be home free. As she should be," I retorted. "Your deputy is overreaching. Interrogating a sleepwalking senior citizen!"

"Morgan Clark is hungry. She's new and wants to make a name for herself in the department. But we must follow the evidence."

"But there's no evidence!"

"We will see. I have to take this in. I am getting a search warrant for the premises. No more rehab until we're done."

"All right!" I threw up my hands, and Don leaned in to brush his lips against mine, and we embraced. He picked up my hand again.

"You should wear the ring." He grimaced.

My mind went to mush while I watched him drive off in his official car.

Chapter 4

While I stood in the foyer, reliving Don's kiss, I saw Eddy's familiar form get out of his pickup and stride up the sidewalk. Eddy Pascal is my ex-husband from fresh out of high school, before I married Jake, whom I lost in a tragic accident. He has slithered around waiting for another opportunity to get back together again for years. I won't go there. But we have become friends, and we have a rent-to-own agreement for my first rehab on Bluebird Street. My first thought at seeing him was that he must have had a spat with Lola.

Eddy stayed on as a renter because his financing fell through for the sale. Which is good and not so good. I wanted to end landlord responsibilities, but Eddy's fiscal responsibility was lacking. As a couple, we hadn't been a good match for a lot of reasons. Mostly because he has the morals of an alley cat. Although he has matured, and I have a soft spot for those days when we were teenagers and in love. Before Lola and others.

"Hey Katie!" As his long lean form approached, I admired the dark, good looks that made me swoon as a teenager. "I thought that was you. I saw the sheriff's car and yours, and I figured you found another house to flip." He threw his arms around me in a bear hug.

"Oh, okay?" Awkwardly, I stepped out of his embrace. "What's new, Eddy?" I had to admit; it was good seeing Eddy. He wasn't complicated. We had history and a friendship that had evolved from fiery passion to a comfortable level of camaraderie.

"Like I said, just cruising by." He looked around the first floor. "Nice place. Looks like it is in good shape. It shouldn't need a lot of work?"

"It doesn't. A little fixing, some disposal of odds and ends, staging, curb appeal, and it should be good to go," I said.

"You don't look too sure." He viewed me. His eyes sparkled, and he brushed a lock of hair from his forehead.

"There's a bit of a glitch."

"Glitch?" He frowned and scratched his head. "How so?"

"I found a gun."

"Whoa. A real gun?" His eyes were wide.

"Yes. It's a long story."

"I've got time." He lifted his shoulders with a big smile.

"Shouldn't you be at work?" Eddy worked in a warehouse. It was a steady job that paid my mortgage on the Bluebird house. He and Lola had an on and off again relationship that I had lost track of what stage it was at. When he saw Don and I were serious, he had made comments about the two of us getting back together. I thought it was a male competition thing and didn't take his overtures to heart.

"I'm off today. Personal day."

"Uh, huh? I am kind of busy right now."

"Wait a minute! This is that guy's house. The one they think killed his co-worker. They showed it on television. It's been all over the news." Even Eddy had heard about the murder. What chance did I have of selling this place? Note to self: pay attention to the newscasts.

Wincing, my shoulders slumped, and my head dropped. "The former owner is a person of interest, but hasn't been charged," I admitted, and added, "Along with another coworker." I hoped to downplay my home seller.

"Katie, you found yourself another murder mystery!" He chortled. When he saw I was not as jovial, he said, "Sorry. It slipped."

"It's okay." I nodded, weary.

"That's why the sheriff was here, right?"

"Yeah, Eddy. It was."

"How's it going with you and the man?" He scanned my face, his lashes lowered, and soft brown eyes sparkled.

"I don't want to talk about it!"

Eddy backed away; his cheerful expression vanished.

"Sure, Katie. I get it. I'm here for you if you want to talk."

"Thanks, Eddy." I was grateful he changed the subject from the trouble that was brewing with the rehab, but talking about Don was taboo, and I felt my blood pressure rise with every reference. I had to face the idea that I didn't know what the heck I was doing with Sheriff Don Williams.

"How are you and Lola?"

"Don't want to talk about it." His gaze traveled over my head.

"You either?" I scanned Eddy's face, which was a mask.

"Nope." He looked at me, his mouth firm. "I will be around if you need any help, Katie. I got time." My nose wrinkled, and I asked, "You're working, right?"

"Yep. Changed my hours, that's all. Nights."

"That is a big change. How do you like it?"

"Pays the bills." He shrugged. I knew what that meant. He was out looking for a job.

"Where's Wayne?" he asked.

I hesitated, not knowing how much Wayne would want me to say about Gillie, but Wayne liked Eddy, and I didn't think he'd mind. Eddy would be in his corner, another support figure for the mess he was facing with Gillie.

"That's another issue." I sighed.

"Okaaay?" he asked with a thoughtful expression.

"He called and said the police were questioning Gillie about her first husband, Walter."

"And?" he asked, looking more puzzled.

"Long story short, she was sleepwalking, and the police picked her up."

"Go on," he prompted.

"She confessed to killing Walter."

"No kidding!"

"Wayne's trying to sort it out with the police. I do not see how they could take what she said seriously. She is an elderly woman who talks in her sleep."

"Me, either. That is unbelievable! Gillie wouldn't hurt a flea."

"I think so, too. But Wayne said she confessed to poisoning Walter."

"What poison?"

"Don't know," I frowned. "I'll talk to Wayne later."

"Let me know what gives," he said. "If you need any help with the rehab, I can fit in a few hours here and there."

"Thanks Eddy. I think I can handle it until Wayne's slate is cleared. It's just some cosmetic work. Won't be too tough."

"Can I take a peek?"

"Sure." I let Eddy pass me in the entry and wander through the family room.

"Nice." He came back around and viewed the kitchen. "Can I go upstairs?" He motioned to the staircase.

"Go for it." I waved him up.

"It looks like the owner did most of the work for you, Katie. Fresh carpet, paint." He called out as he climbed the stairs to the second floor, and I followed.

"Yep, it's pretty clean. I think he would have finished everything, but I came along and made him an offer, as is. And he took it."

"Good job." He finished his tour of the upstairs and met me in the hall. "You always had a knack for money and houses and stuff. You always had a project going, even when we were kids. I remember the curtains you made." He smiled. We couldn't afford much, and I had bought fabric and sewed window treatments on an ancient Singer machine for the tall narrow windows in our apartment.

"Thanks, Eddy." I tilted my head in his direction, glancing at him, and led him downstairs. "I appreciate it." I muttered to myself, "Wish my fiancé felt the same way," and I lingered in the entry while he made another pass of the first floor.

"What?" he asked. Lost in thought, he studied the house. The kitchen was at the far end, with the family/living room open to the dining and kitchen area. The staircase was to the left; behind that and to the left of the kitchen was a powder room. A door that led to the garage was to the right of the main entry. He ambled back to the foyer. Opening the garage door, he peered inside. "Nice big garage, too." He shut the door and looked at me. "Did you say something?"

"It was nothing." I bit my lip and left out the front door.

"Huh, okay." He followed me and stood, zipping his jacket while I locked the door. "Gotta go. It was great seeing you, Katie." And he swooped in, his lips brushing my forehead and leaving me breathless. My mind had gone to mush with Don's visit, and now again with Eddy. As he drove off, a whirl of emotions washed over me. Eddy was still handsome, and life with him had held passion mingled with a chaos that became predictable. A future with Don felt solid, but meant change, the unknown.

Chapter 5

Later that night at home, I called Myra. I had eaten dinner, showered, dressed in sweats, and slipped on the beautiful ring. Boots had taken residence on the back of the sofa, grooming himself as I parked my computer on the coffee table.

"There's a lot going on, Myra."

"Tell me about it," she urged.

"I called Don, and he shut down the rehab again this morning." I hesitated, "I found a gun."

"No way!" She inhaled.

"Yep. He's going to check for the owner of the weapon and search the house again."

"Bummer."

"Wayne called, Gillie's in jail."

"What on earth for?" she exclaimed.

"She confessed to killing her first husband while she was sleepwalking. Wayne's beside himself. He didn't work today."

"I don't believe she did any such thing."

"I don't either."

"Then Eddy came by."

"Oh, boy." She groaned. "What did he want?"

"He's working nights, said if I needed any help with the project, he could help."

"So, Lola's working during the day, and he's at loose ends?"

"Maybe?" I said, wrinkling my nose. I could not figure out what Eddy was up to.

"And you're having second thoughts about marrying Don," she said, a note of dismay in her voice.

"You nailed it," I confessed.

"You need a reading."

"A what?"

"A reading with a psychic. Sort things out."

"Like a tarot card reading? Isn't that kind of dicey? Won't that open a portal to the dark side?" Myra and I had a tentative sense of the paranormal. I had encouraged an other-worldly view with our first flip where I had discovered a dead body, and we'd had a sage burning to clear the house. We'd had a cleansing ritual with sage and candles in every house since then. Myra had surprised me by going further because she was so grounded. At my rehab in Hiptown, she had engaged a ghost buster named Bernie who officiated weddings and had performed Wayne and Gillie's nuptials. The seniors had had a commitment ceremony in Las Vegas but made their union legit in a welcome home reception in their new home. Bernie drove for Uber as well. We all have to pay the bills.

"It doesn't have to be tarot. There are other cards, if the traditional ones look imposing. Or just a reading."

"You're really into this?"

"It is a tool. Like counseling without the 'how does that make you feel' interrogation." She chuckled. I knew all about counseling after Jake, my ex, died unexpectedly. Therapy had been helpful, but exhausting and painful.

"All right." That sounded like the sane Myra I knew and could rely on. If it did not involve a long, drawn-out examination of my psyche, I could get on board.

In the hall that ran the length of the units, I heard voices.

"Hang on, Myra," I said, and I put the phone to my shoulder, straining to make out the conversation. I couldn't make out the words, but the overall tone was Wayne comforting Gillie, and then I heard the door open to their unit. It once belonged to a tenant who died, and whose unit Wayne and I rehabbed. Gillie and Wayne purchased the refreshed unit as their together home. "It sounds like Wayne just brought Gillie home." I rose and peeked out at the patio. Lights reflected from the unit to the courtyard outside.

"Do you think she killed her first husband?" Myra asked.

"No way. She was dreaming. She can't be responsible for anything she says."

"But what went on in that house if she dreamed of killing her husband?" She sounded thoughtful, musing over their dilemma.

"Huh?" Myra brought up a subject I had never considered. I had believed Gillie's marriage to Walter was solid, with no reason to think otherwise. Gillie had always been a private person, and her earlier marriage hadn't been a topic of conversation. But what if the union hadn't been happy or solid?

"She's never talked a lot about her life with Walter, but I don't believe she killed him."

Rat-a-tat-tat!

I jumped, hearing Wayne's signature knock at the door.

"I have to go, Wayne's here. This could take a while."

"Let me know what happened," she said. "Call me."

"You know I will."

I hung up and opened the door to a disheveled Wayne. His face drawn, his blue eyes, normally twinkling with mirth, were dull. His long gray hair was back, tucked behind his ears. He stooped as he spoke. "Hey, Kiddo. Wanted to let you know I sprung Gillie."

"Thanks, Wayne. Come in?"

"For just a minute, don't want to leave Gillie too long." I motioned to the easy chair in the living room. He sank down heavily, gripping the arms of the chair. "She's asleep right now."

"Can I get you something to drink?"

"Nope. Nothing." He shook his head.

"How is she?" I sat on the sofa across from him.

"Kind of shook up." His mouth twisted. "We both are."

"What happened?"

"She just plumb got up one night. I was asleep. She got dressed and walked outside, still sleeping."

"She undid the deadbolt locks and chain, too?" I frowned. He had installed more locks the first time Gillie left the unit they shared while he slept. One time Wayne came over harried, while Myra was visiting, and we'd gone out to search for her, only to find she had been homesick and gone to her unit. They had tried counseling. Her doctor had suggested a medication that Gillie had been on, but she didn't want to use the drug again because it made her groggy the next day.

"Yeah, wearing one of her outfits." He smiled. "The lavender pants and hoodie get-up. Left her hair in curlers." He chuckled. I smiled at the image of Gillie, now Gretta Hamer, wearing one of her hallmark sweats outfits and the pink sponge curlers she habitually wore to style her fine hair.

"So, the police took her to the station?"

"Yep. She didn't have any identification on her, and she wouldn't give her address," he said.

"Then what happened?"

"The new deputy, Clark, saw she wasn't quite right, but couldn't wake her. Asked her more questions, and Gillie just spouted out that she killed Walter with tea from a poison plant, named Monkshood. That's when it got crazy."

"I'll bet." My brows furrowed.

"Clark brought Gillie into the station and questioned her. She repeated that she had given Walter tea brewed from the plant. Clark put her in a cell and let her sleep. She asked for me when she woke up. The deputy said she could leave, but that she would have to check out her story. She asked her about Monkshood, and Gillie avowed it was one of her favorites in the perennial garden. It was such a pretty blue. But she had no memory of her confession."

"Oh, my." My stomach dipped. "So, now they have to check out her story, because she grows the plant." My knowledge of plants was minimal, having killed many in my attempt to nurture a garden. I wouldn't know a Monkshood from any other blue flowering plant. Well, except a petunia. Gillie was an avid gardener, and her patio and garden were clear evidence of her love of nature.

"Walter died from heart failure, right?"

"Yep. Massive heart attack is what the doctors told Gillie."

"They'll check the death certificate and see it's all a big mistake."

"Hope so. Gillie sure is upset." He shook his head and grimaced.

"I don't blame her." I winced. "Should she be alone?"

"I locked the door. We'll keep an ear out."

"That'll work." It was both a boon and a problem that the hallway connecting the townhomes could be noisy with people coming and going.

"I want to take a few days with Gillie and get this mess straightened out," he said.

"No problem. You look like you could use some 'me' time, too?"

"Yep. We'll take a day trip, see how spring is shaping up in a different part of the state." It was early March, and signs of spring were about, with warming temperatures and the tree's leafing out. Crocus Heights was in the middle of Minnesota, with reports of the southern part of the state warming fast.

"A change of scenery would be good for both of you." I smiled agreeably.

"How's the new job going?" he asked.

"It's going." I shrugged, avoiding eye contact.

"Is something up?" He frowned.

"Nothing to fret about." I shook my head, gazing absently at Boots who wandered to my feet, shaking his tail.

"Huh?" He tilted his head.

"No worries," I said. "It's okay, really."

"Kiddo, you're making me worry."

"There's been a situation." I bit my lower lip, not wanting Wayne to feel guilty about taking time with Gillie.

"What?" He rubbed his chin and frowned.

"I found a gun hidden in the fireplace mantel."

"A gun? Someone must have been in a big hurry to sell the house to forget their gun." He guffawed. He saw I didn't laugh, and he quit, his expression sober. "What's the story?"

"The man who sold it to me, Sean Young, is a person of interest in a murder case. Another coworker, Nathan Winner, was named too. The three men were all up for the same promotion, but Arthur Cook got the job, and was found dead with a gunshot wound."

"Whoa! That big case? The one where they found the guy in a field?"

"Yes." I studied Wayne. Even with his problems with Gillie, he knew about this case. I must really be in a funk, living in a bubble.

"Is there something else?" He saw my pensive look.

"No. There's just a lot going on with Don and being engaged, and now the rehab is hot mess. He didn't want me to take on another renovation. But it is what I do." I shrugged. "You have got enough happening with Gillie, Wayne. No need to add to the load."

"No problem, Kiddo. I got broad shoulders," he joked. "Seriously, it's all an adventure, all in the journey."

"Myra said the same thing." I studied him thoughtfully.

"Myra's a smart lady. I better get back to Gillie." I walked him to the door.

"Take all the time you need. The investigators have to search the house again. I can't do any work until they're done."

"Thanks. It will all work out." He winked and left with a nod.

Chapter 6

"You had to rip apart the whole place?" I wailed. Don stood beside me, his hands tucked into his pants pockets and his face grim. We stood at the top of the staircase in the hall outside of the owner's suite for the renovation. The new carpeting had been torn up, showing bare wood, and thread remnants from the tears littered the floor.

"Yep. Had to check the carpet backing and subfloor for blood evidence." He shifted his feet and studied the floor.

"The police couldn't have done this when Sean Young owned the house?"

"We didn't have probable cause for a warrant to search the premises then. Can't search without a warrant. Sean Young was a person of interest, but not the only person on the radar. Arthur Cook wasn't popular, and there was another man vying for the same promotion."

"Who?"

"Another coworker, Nathan Winner. I only told you because his name is out there."

"Okay." I feigned ignorance that I'd heard there was someone else police were looking at.

"That's all you get," Don warned. "No snooping." He sighed and muttered, "And that's like waving a red flag in front of a charging bull."

I dimly heard his grousing as a chill traveled my spine while viewing the red, brownish splotch, which I assumed was blood, stretched across the bedroom entry, with more spots down the staircase from the primary bedroom to the first level.

"What a mess," I muttered. The new carpet and paint job was a total loss. The place was a disaster.

"Why?" I had expected the fireplace to be dismantled, but the entire house?

"The investigators were following up on a lead."

"What tip?" I braced myself, waiting for him to say, "Can't comment on an ongoing investigation." It was refreshing to hear, "Again, you're likely to hear what I'm about to tell you on the news."

"What is it?" I waited, frowning.

"The suspect's wife told her co-workers that she was happy that she and Sean had found a new house. But that he had repainted and replaced the carpet. She thought the money should be spent in their new home, and she was upset he had done the work while she was away visiting her mother. After interviewing the coworkers, we were cleared to search the premises. That was enough to get a warrant." He cleared his throat. "Plus, you found a gun."

"Yeah, I did." Curses, I should have kept my mouth shut. Then, no, you can't ignore a gun. Even if you have been in a fog, out of touch with the news, and making major life changes. I gazed at Don. He was handsome with blond hair dotted with silver, and he was serious, stable, and everything a woman should want. Why was I in such a tizzy?

"Hello? Anyone here?" Myra called from the entry, holding the door ajar.

"Up here, Myra," I called. She entered the house and halted.

"Oh, dear." She looked up the staircase at us. "It's a wreck."

We trekked downstairs, meeting her on the landing.

"The investigators did a thorough search." He pursed his lips. "I will let you two talk. Kate, I'll call later. We could have dinner?" He asked, watching my expression.

"Sure." Dinner out always brightened my day.

He grinned and patted my arm.

"Later. Good to see you, Myra." He gave a quick smile and nodded as he passed her on the way out. She returned his nod, "Yes, sheriff," she replied and observed his departing form. Her eyes twinkled when she met mine.

"Katelyn, he is such a nice man."

"Yes, he is." I grimaced. "Except for wanting me to give up my home, my business, and now my budget is shot fixing this mess. Argh."

"There's a bit of turbulence right now." She was circumspect, her voice soothing. "It is a big change. Have you two had time to talk?"

"No." I shook my head. "Maybe tonight."

"You'll be fine." She surveyed the premises. "But it looks like there'll be more work than you expected."

"It's trashed," I said, flatly. With my hands on my hips, I surveyed the damages. "All the carpet in the primary bedroom and down the staircase is shredded. The walls have black marks where they ripped up the carpet, and it hit the walls. The air ducts were removed, and now they're marred."

"Carpet and paint." Myra said. "Not so bad. Wayne can do the mantel when he's free."

"Yeah, I guess you're right. Been there, done that. I can do it again." I shook my head and met her gaze. "It was supposed to be an easy redo."

"It's disappointing." She nodded.

"It is." I shrugged.

"So, you're going to dinner with Don tonight?"

"That's the plan."

"That will be good. You'll have fun and some quality time together."

"I guess," I muttered.

"And Gillie is home," she mused.

"Myra, I don't know if I can marry Don." I let out a breath that was stuck in my chest.

"Don't say that. It is pre-wedding jitters, that's all."

"I don't know if I can marry anyone again," I confessed.

"Oh, that's different." She viewed me through lowered lids. "I think we should have that reading sooner rather than later. It might give you some clarity."

"Yes. Sooner is better."

"I'll set it up."

"With whom?" I blinked, frowning.

"I know somebody." She winked. "Don't worry."

"Sounds good." I chuckled and turned to the chaos in the house. "It'll take a few hours to clean this mess. That will take care of the afternoon. Wayne is with Gillie."

"How is she?" Myra asked.

"I haven't seen her yet. Wayne came over last night to tell me he and Gillie needed a break, and they're planning a trip. They're both shook up."

"A break will be good for them. I must go." She checked her watch. "Got an appointment with my hairdresser."

"Your hair looks good. Mine should look that good," I said, smoothing down my dark brown unmanageable mane. Myra was always perfectly groomed. Today, she wore a black fleece warm-up jacket with a colorful scarf, sharp black jeans, and polished nails. My work outfit consisted of whatever sweatshirt and jeans I found first. Manicures were questionable, at best.

"Heavens, I can't stand it. Need a cut, the color is off." At fifty-five, she was 20 years my senior, and people asked if we were sisters. We could be. Hopefully, I looked like the younger sister.

"We'll talk soon." With a nod, she headed to her black SUV parked in the driveway. Slipping on a pair of work gloves, I secured the door behind me. Don had cautioned me to lock up while working alone, and I followed the advice as much as possible.

Opening the door from the entry to the attached garage, I pulled up the damaged carpeting and hauled it to the garage. It could stay there until I ordered a dumpster. My major task that day was to clear the space. While I worked, I mulled over dinner. The prospect of spending time with him made me smile. Myra was right. It was pre-wedding nerves. We had not set a date or discussed venues. It was his first marriage, my third. Both of my earlier ceremonies had been casual affairs. With no parents to advise, Eddy and I had eloped. Jake and I had taken our vows in the backyard of our new home. While I pondered the possibilities, I muttered, "Let's just get through dinner tonight."

Chapter 7

I went back to work, hauling out the damaged flooring, and jumped when the overhead garage door creaked open. Whirling, I faced the visitor. It was Sean Young.

"Sorry, didn't mean to scare you." He shielded his eyes as he peered inside.

"You have a remote?!" I gasped.

"Yeah. I wanted to return it. The door is locked, but I saw your car in the drive." He nodded over his shoulder at my very capable gray Ford Escape, circa 1998. Frowning, he saw the stack of flooring in the garage. "That's the new carpet. What gives?"

"The police searched the house again."

"What for?" His expression turned into a glower.

"Evidence." My brows lifted, and I noted his pallor had turned to a gray.

"That I killed Arthur Cook?"

"Yep." I faced Sean and watched his face as he went through a series of emotions. The first was anger and confusion, acceptance, then resolve.

"I didn't kill Arthur. He was a dickwad, but I did not kill him." His tone held a warning. "I let them search the house because I am innocent. They didn't have a warrant. The police asked, and I consented. I have nothing to hide."

"I found a gun." I said, watching his face. "That triggered another search. They found dried blood under the carpet."

"Gun. What gun?"

"A three fifty-seven revolver, hidden in the mantel."

"It isn't mine." Annoyed, he shook his head. "The blood is mine. I broke a glass in the primary bathroom, stepped in the shards, and started bleeding. The first aid kit was in the powder room downstairs. I tried to stem the blood, but it soaked through the towel while I walked."

"All right." I wiped drops of perspiration from my forehead.

"That was why I had the new carpet installed. It wasn't the smartest move I've ever made, but I have this condition and I had to move fast."

"What condition?" I faced him, my hands on my hips.

"I'm a hemophiliac. I gush blood when I get cut. It's rare, and there is no cure."

"You didn't have a first aid kit in the primary bath or bedroom?" If it were me, I would carry a first aid kit everywhere I went.

"We were getting ready to move. It was packed, and I didn't want to dig through boxes."

"Okay." I relaxed.

"So, when they test the blood, it's mine. It is not Arthur's."

"Why do you say Arthur was a jerk?"

"He was always taking credit for other people's work. Schmoozing with the bosses. Making himself look like the hero, when it was other people who did the work and kept silent. I kept quiet and tried to be his friend."

"Do you think it was somebody from Maxim's that killed him?"

"Could be. Could have been his girlfriend who did him in."

"Why his girlfriend?"

"They were engaged, and the rumor was, he slept around."

"Oh!" I was surprised. I hadn't heard Arthur was engaged, or that he was cheating on his soon-to-be wife.

"I doubt she would have killed him, though."

"Why not?"

"She was the sweetest gal ever, brought him food or coffee when he worked late. She adored him, blinded by love. Poor gal."

"Hum." It sounded like me with Eddy, the blinded by love part. Thank goodness I had met and married Jake after our disastrous union. Don was solid, too.

"Here's the garage door opener." He held it out. "Sorry I scared you, but I didn't kill Arthur, and I don't know who did."

"Uh, huh."

I watched Sean drive away in a dark blue minivan. Aiming the remote, I closed the overhead door and slipped the gizmo into my jacket pocket. Heading back inside, I resumed pulling carpeting into the garage.

I recalled he'd said at the closing that his wife had an opener. They had taken one car to the meeting and had forgotten a second remote in another car. I had not done my due diligence and changed the codes, or the locks. Chalk one up for Sean and honesty. I hadn't known about the murder at the time of the closing and wasn't suspicious of him. Now, with the knowledge there was an unsolved murder and Sean Young was under suspicion, my attitude had changed, and I was on high alert. Selling a house where a violent crime had taken place required full disclosure, plus it was bad karma.

My mind wandered to the evening ahead with Don. Our first since we had the snit about our future home. Could we do what Wayne and Gillie had done, take on another residence for the two of us, and put off the decision? Some couples never live together. Was that a solution?

We could change off living in each other's homes on a monthly or weekly basis. Somehow, that didn't sit well. That seemed to be the lifestyle of a high-powered couple with multiple residences and big incomes. Not that Don was any slouch, but that wasn't me. I wanted a home for the two of us. One that we both chose. With that in mind, I finished hauling the rest of the carpet to the garage and swept up the debris left behind.

I locked up, uneasy about Sean's unexpected visit. I hoped that would be the last of him, and felt a little smug about telling Don that I already knew the blood stains were Sean's.

Chapter 8

"Let me get this straight, Katelyn. Sean Young stopped at the rehab while you were doing your flipping thing and left a garage door opener he could have sent by mail." Don's tone was loud and firm, and his deep cobalt eyes flickered anger, while he read me the riot act.

"It is not a 'thing,' it's my livelihood!" I felt my face turn red.

"Yes. Of course." Don lowered his volume and rubbed his forehead. "I'm sorry. I don't mean to be rude."

"Hum."

"I worry about you working at the houses alone. It was nervy of this guy to use the opener."

"It was." I conceded. "He said he knocked, but no one answered. So, he opened the garage door."

"What was he going to do if no one was in the garage? Enter the house?" Don's usually calm demeanor bordered on highly irritated, and his voice rose with the question.

"We didn't get into that. Maybe would have left the opener outside the door?" I shook my head and surveyed the evening dinner crowd at Joseph's. It was his favorite place to dine. The food was heavenly. The well-heeled patrons relaxed in the dining room with white tablecloths, cloth napkins, and rich oiled woodwork. Don wore a dinner jacket with a light-yellow shirt open at the neck. He looked at ease in the richly appointed surroundings. I wore a simple black sweater with black slacks. The servers wore black as well. Another clothing faux pas on my part.

"Katelyn," he grabbed my hands and ran a finger over the diamond engagement ring. "This man has not been cleared of murder. I don't like this business. When is Wayne going to be back?"

"I don't know. It's hard with Gillie. They have to check her deceased husband's death certificate, but I am sure it will be fine."

"I agree." He sipped wine and gazed at me over the rim of his glass.

"He wants to take a trip. Visit the southern part of the state."

"He should." He nodded, his mouth firm. "They haven't charged her, but police may want her to stay close to home. It may have to be a staycation. She likes plants. She would enjoy the Conservatory?"

"Maybe not there." My eyes widened. "Plants could be a touchy subject."

He winced. "Sorry, my bad. Day trip should be fine. Can't believe they think it could have been a poison made from her flowers." He shook his head and sipped his wine.

"Uh, huh." I cleared my throat and said, "Eddy stopped by. He offered to work during the day. He's working nights."

"Eddy?" His brows rose, skeptical, his head tilted.

"What? You don't trust Eddy or me?" I met his gaze.

"I trust you." He set his wineglass down and sat back, his eyes searching.

"So, it's Eddy?" Unnerved, I twisted the napkin in my lap, hidden from his view.

"Katelyn, Eddy's a bit unreliable." That I couldn't disagree with.

"You don't think he'd do any work?" I reached for the glass of water on the table.

"Maybe." He cleared his throat.

"Maybe what?" I frowned and took a sip.

It was then the server swooped in with our food, and we dug in, each of us savoring a bite of our main dish. Mine was salmon, and his, a steak, each with mashed potatoes and grilled asparagus.

"I want you to stay with me while you're rehabbing the house."

"I can't leave Boots alone," I protested.

"Bring Boots. It will be a good opportunity for him to get comfortable in an unfamiliar environment." He paused and studied me.

"Not during the week. It is too far to travel every day." Don's mansion was close to Joseph's, about a half hour drive from Crocus Heights and my rehab projects. It had a wonderful view of the lake, boasted an enormous swimming pool, a groomed lawn, and an immense garage. "And there is always work on the weekends as well. It is easier if I stay put with Boots. "

"You're one tough cookie, Katelyn." He sighed, and sat back, sated with the sumptuous food.

The server swooped in again, cleared the table of dinner plates, and left a dessert menu.

He took the menu. "Speaking of cookies, how about dessert?"

"I shouldn't." I said and patted my stomach.

"But I will." He ordered a hot fudge sundae and two spoons. The sweets came, and he took a bite of the gooey hot fudge and ice cream.

"By the way, do you have any news about the blood under the carpet?" I asked, batting my lashes.

"You know I can't talk about an ongoing investigation." He was firm.

I'd expected as much. He offered me a spoonful of ice cream, fudge, and whipped topping. Accepting the bite, I picked up the second spoon and dug in. Debating whether to tell him about my conversation with Sean, I opted for silence. A tiny piece of me wanted to spill what Sean had told me about his condition.

Instead, I suggested, "You could stay at my place?" At his raised eyebrows, I added, "There is a spare room."

"I will consider it. I'm used to a routine. Esther making breakfast, doing my laundry."

"No breakfast service. I make a great cup of coffee. You do your own laundry."

"Once again, a hard bargain." He smiled.

"Boots is amenable to snuggles," I added.

"I hope you'd provide the snuggles," he teased, with a twinkle in his eyes.

"It's possible." I smiled and took another spoonful of the sundae.

Chapter 9

It had been a wonderful evening with Don, but it was back to reality the next morning at the rehab. In my haste to start the day, I had left my ring on. Slipping it off, I stashed it in my jeans pocket. Nervously, I felt for the gem between tasks to be sure it stayed deep within the pocket.

I finished hauling the carpet to the garage and cleaning up the area.

The doorbell rang while I measured the area for the new flooring. I answered the door and saw Eddy's profile.

"Hey, Eddy." I frowned. He faced me with a glum expression.

"I'm free today, Katie. Thought you might need some help?" He sounded hopeful and a little sheepish.

"I'm having a dumpster delivered this morning. If you want to stick around and load the container with the old carpet and pad?"

"That'd be great." He brightened. "You look good Katie, you glow."

"Thanks, Eddy." I opened the door for him.

"Don't see a ring," he stepped inside and glanced at my hand.

"I can't wear it at the rehab." What was it with men and rings? My mind slipped to when we were married and wore matching gold bands purchased from a discount store. We couldn't afford more than that, and it had been enough.

"There's coffee in a thermos in the kitchen."

"Awesome!" He grinned. "How's it going with Wayne and Gillie?" He followed me to the kitchen, where I poured coffee into the thermos cup and offered it.

"Wayne's taking Gillie on a day trip. Give them a break from the investigation."

"Wouldn't it be something if Gillie did in her ex?"

"It would, but she didn't." I was firm.

"You just never know. She seems like a sweet lady, but you can never be sure about people."

"Stop it. She did not do anything. They would have charged her if there was proof."

My cell phone rang, and I dug it out of my pocket.

"Hi Wayne," I answered while Eddy, with cup in hand, wandered through the first floor. Dimly, I heard him open the garage access door. "What's up? Where are you folks headed?"

"Gillie's in jail again. They're holding her for 48 hours while they investigate Walter's death."

"No!"

"Yep. They said that Monkshood has a chemical, aconitine, that acts in the body like a heart attack. Walter did not have any record of heart disease. Healthy as a horse, that Clark woman says." I didn't know Morgan Clark but recalled that Don had said she was young and ambitious.

"Unbelievable!" I sputtered. "Walter may not have a medical record for heart disease, but that doesn't mean he didn't have heart issues."

"Gillie said he didn't go to the doctor regularly. But they got her on tape confessing."

"She was sleepwalking!"

"Tell it to that new detective, Clark." Wayne sounded resigned.

"How are they going to prove she didn't do it?" I pondered.

"They could exhume the body," he said.

"Oh. My. God."

"I have got to go. Gotta check on a lawyer. Wanted to keep you in the loop. It's going to be a while before I can do anything at the rehab. Sorry."

"No apologies, Wayne. It will all be fine."

"Sure hope so. What a mess!"

I hung up from Wayne, stunned, and blurted to Eddy, who had returned from his meandering, and was pouring himself another cup of java.

"They arrested Gillie! I am going to call Don and see what the heck is going on."

Hastily, I dialed.

"Katelyn, calm down." Don's even temper fueled mine.

"I can't! You are taking advantage of a senior citizen who was sleepwalking when she confessed to a murder. We all know she didn't do it!"

"We have to investigate suspicious deaths. Even when it is Gillie. No one is above the law."

"Walter died of a heart attack! Let her go."

"Katelyn, the truth will come out. I can't discuss an open case, and this conversation is ended."

"Why isn't this Clark woman investigating Arthur Brett Cook's murder? That was Sean's blood in the house, not Arthur's," I blurted.

There was silence. Don's voice was even, with a steely undertone, "How would you know that?"

After a minute that felt like an eternity, I mumbled, "He told me."

"Sean Young told you it was his blood, not Arthur's." His voice was flat.

"Yes. He did." I was defiant now.

"What else did he tell you? And I will remind you not to hinder a police investigation."

Chastised, I related our conversation.

"He said Arthur took credit for other people's work, and that he was having an affair with a married woman. He was not well-liked."

"We are aware of Arthur's reputation. Katelyn, stay out of it."

"I have to go. Eddy's here. He's going to help me today with the rehab."

"Eddy?" He sounded curt. Sensing that I hit a nerve, I hung up.

"Hey Katie, trouble in paradise?" Eddy's eyebrows raised. Hiding a grin, he sipped his coffee.

"Never mind." Hearing the rumble of the roll-off dumpster delivery in the drive, I went to the garage. I raised the overhead door, okayed the drop location, and waved off the driver. Agitated by the morning's chaos, I started tossing carpet and pad into the container. Eddy joined me after a minute's hesitation, and together we made quick work of filling the dumpster.

Calmed by the exertion, I breathed easier, brushed my hair back, and said, "Thanks, Eddy."

"No problem." He straightened and rubbed his lower back. "Glad to help."

We viewed the container filled with the remnants.

"Too bad it was trashed in the search," Eddy said.

"Yeah. It's a shame. It was good carpet." I agreed, nodding. "I'm going to head over to the home store and order new flooring."

"Do you want company?" Eddy asked.

"No. You've done enough this morning. I owe you." Eddy wasn't a shopper. He was a buyer on a beer budget with champagne tastes. I wanted affordable and no discussion.

"No problem. Anytime. Hope it works out with Gillie. It'd be funny if she did the deed." I stared at Eddy. He backpedaled at my glare. "But she probably didn't." His brown eyes sparkled, and he smothered a grin.

"Eddy, it isn't funny."

"Nope. It isn't." He sobered up. "Catcha later." He strolled to his truck and waved goodbye.

Chapter 10

I lowered the door and went inside to grab my messenger bag and checked to see I had the measurements. Satisfied that the slip of paper was safe in the black hole of receipts, color swatches, and papers in my bag, I headed to my vehicle. I had opted for a smaller Ford SUV this time around when I traded off my yellow hatchback. It sat higher, with more space for hauling supplies, and it blended in with all the other gray vehicles. It was the nicest car I'd owned in my career as a home rehab specialist, or ever, and was a pleasant change being inconspicuous on the road.

I started toward the home store and then made an abrupt turn to the police station. Still seething that Gillie was behind bars, I had to speak to this ambitious new detective. But first, I wanted to grill Don about Morgan Clark.

On my way past the beauty shop, shoe store, variety store, laundry, and bank building that made up the drive to the station, I calmed myself with pleasant thoughts of my evening with Don. He had balked at staying at my house, and I wasn't amenable to moving in with him. That meant we had to find our own place. Not so different from Wayne and Gillie, who had opted for the third unit in my complex. His, hers, and theirs.

Maybe that was causing Gillie's sleepwalking? They had not committed to their place. I wasn't a psychologist. All I knew was that she would not have killed her Walter. Gillie may be nosy and an eavesdropper, but she was not a killer.

Parking across the street from the station, I threw open the heavy double doors with an attitude. Directed to have a seat by the attendant, I cooled my heels seated on a hard wooden chair while she called the sheriff.

The staff had grown since my last meeting with Don at his workplace. Now they had a woman seated at a desk behind a glass partition who greeted the public, and of course, the new detective, Morgan Clark. They had updated the pictures of the staff, and while I waited, I studied the picture of said detective.

She looked fierce. Her bright blue eyes peered out, and a slight sneer shaded her face. She had short cropped blonde hair. Her heft was apparent with a thick neck and squared shoulders.

"You can go in now," the woman behind the partition called. I headed into the sheriff's office, where he sat at his desk, studying his monitor, one hand gripping a pen to take notes on a yellow legal pad.

"Katelyn. What brings you here?" A smile stretched across his face; his eyes lit up. He sat back from his computer and released the pen.

"I want to talk to Morgan Clark." His smile evened out and his expression grew serious. His shoulders tensed, and he reached for his coffee mug.

"Why?" He straightened, gripped the cup, and held my stare.

"I want to speak to the person who is holding Gillie on a nonsensical idea."

"There's nothing you can do about Gillie. The investigation must run its course. Besides, she is unavailable right now." His cool gaze and manner held me at bay.

"She's out charging more seniors with crimes they didn't commit?" I snapped. The "be reasonable," sheriff style hadn't comforted me, and added to my frustration.

"Calm down. She is out on a call."

He straightened in his swivel chair and placed both palms on the desk. "She's not a bad deputy." He raised his hands in caution. "Honest."

His soothing manner prevailed, and I relented.

"When will they let Gillie go?"

"After their investigation. They will check into her disposition at the time of the confession and review the medical records."

"I thought they already did that."

"They want to run more toxicology reports."

"All right. Then she will be free to go?"

"We will let her go as soon as it is determined that Walter died of natural causes."

I calmed down, with the assurance that Gillie would be released as quickly as possible. What else could I do? Wayne was standing by her and that would help her through this mess. I had a house to rehab and carpeting to buy. Don walked me to the door, and squeezed my shoulder reassuringly, while the woman who attended the front desk watched us furtively. I went on my way.

***

The Home Store had a deal on free installation for carpet over a certain amount. I snapped it up, along with the earliest install date they had available - Thursday, the following week. Until then, I would get the rest of the mess cleared out and do whatever cleaning was needed.

The roll-off dumpster awaited the rest of the debris from the house. While I emptied items from cabinets--mismatched glassware, Christmas tins, and the like--I considered Sean's comment about Arthur canoodling with the receptionist at Maxim's. The woman in question was married at the time of the infidelity. I wanted to check out Arthur's fiancé and finagle whatever I could about the alleged affair. The third person up for the promotion, Nathan Winner, was still an unknown.

While I pondered how I might find Arthur's fiancé, Myra called. Her voice was high and lilting with excitement, and she said, "I have a woman, a psychic, who can tell whether the changes in your life are in your best interest."

"Really?" I checked the time. "It's nearly five o'clock. How about we meet at Ivan's and have a bite? You can tell me all about her."

Inwardly, I groaned. I didn't want to talk to anyone about my qualms about marrying again, especially a fortune teller. What if the woman saw danger ahead? What then?

If I dwelled on how my life would change, it added to the queasy feeling about my upcoming nuptials. I had to stay busy, nose into Gillie's predicament, see what happened with Sean. Was he off the hook for Arthur's death? All those questions avoided the current situation with Don and merging our lives. It felt safer solving a murder. I knew Myra had my best interest at heart, so I'd suck it up and find out what this woman was all about. I was inquisitive, too, about what a psychic might say about my future. Queasy, but curious.

Myra was already seated when I breezed into Ivan's. I had spotted her sleek, black SUV in the parking lot. Ivan and Maggie, the owners, waved me into the dining room while they checked out customers at the front counter. I peeked around the Russian immigrant-owned cafe without the help of Katarina, their feisty server/manager.

I spotted Myra in a booth and slipped onto the bench across from her. She had a cat-ate-the-canary look, which I ignored while I settled into the hard seat, until I couldn't evade her expression any longer.

"So, tell me about this psychic?" I asked, my back stiff against the booth.

It was then Katarina made her presence known with menus, and a curt, "What you want to drink?" Myra and I exchanged tight smiles. I said, "Coffee." Myra added, "Me too. Make mine decaf."

"You ready to order food?" The dark-haired server snipped.

"Sure."

We knew Ivan's menu by heart, and we ordered the Ivan Burgers with all the trimmings, and French fries to boot. It would not be a carb free, low-cal event for either of us. I needed carbs to soothe the nerves I had about visiting a psychic and asking her about my life.

"Where's your ring?" Myra asked, frowning after the server.

"Oops." I dug the ring out of my jeans pocket and slipped it on.

"Careful. You don't want to lose it. It is breathtaking."

"Yes. It is," I said. We gazed at the diamond for a moment, and Myra said. "The psychic's name is Gabriella. She is of Roma Hungarian descent and reads people's cards in Hiptown. Her people immigrated to the United States in the last century. She comes very well recommended."

"By whom?"

"Bernie, of course."

"Why not ask Bernie to read?"

"He doesn't read Tarot cards. His expertise is in ghost busting."

"Everyone has a specialty," I said. Smirking, my brows rose.

"Don't be a skeptic. We all have our strong suits. She reads palms too."

"Hmm. A palm reading could be an option. It may be a safer alternative to the tarot cards with the depiction of a hanged man, or darker scenes." I didn't want to invite any bad karma, and a palm shouldn't be too dark. The skeptic inside was a little scared of getting a reading filled with ominous warnings.

"Of course, a palm reading would be perfect! But there are different decks of Tarot, with less dire pictures. It is all in the interpretation," she said with a smile.

"All right. I will try to keep an open mind. Where does this woman give readings?"

"There is a spacious old Victorian residence on the main drag of Hiptown. It's across from a pizza joint."

"I know where it is!" I had spied the colorful mansion with the outside veranda advertising for psychic connections on many trips to the most delicious pizzeria around. "That's the house across from the Pizza Factory!"

"Yes. She does readings on the terrace in the summer months, and there is a four-season porch with full-length windows that she uses during the winter. She believes in working in the public sphere, to offset the ooky spooky attached to psychic readings. Transparency."

"What if you don't want to be seen having your cards or palm read?"

Myra looked at me. "Is there something you're hiding?"

"Well, no. Maybe? Who knows?" I stammered. "I am a private person, and I like to keep a low profile. Besides, what if the sheriff drives by? How would that look? That pizza place is a hangout for the cops."

"Hum, that is unlikely," she said brightly, "But, we can wear disguises. A wig, different clothes."

"Myra, that's genius." I held my cup up in a toast. "Let's do it."

Myra agreed to set up the readings with Gabriella, and I left with a burning desire to find the receptionist at Maxim's and ask a few questions about my other quest. Who killed Arthur Brett Cook? Myra didn't know it, but she had given me an idea for finding the woman who was allegedly having a fling with Arthur at the time of his murder.

Chapter 11

That evening at home, I rummaged through my closet for the wig left from my gypsy costume from the last Halloween. Boots sat on the bed, eyeing my search with interest. I found the faux hair stuffed in a box along with the costume.

"Aha!" I chortled and slipped it on. Boots looked dismayed. Gazing into the mirror, I realized why I had never worn it. It was obviously fake and only meant to be worn on Halloween. The gypsy outfit had been attractive with the full skirt and fitted bodice, but the hair not so much. It would attract more attention than if I kept my dark, unkempt locks. I would have to go a different route with a disguise to fool a psychic, not to mention a corporate receptionist.

Rat-a-tat-tat! It was Wayne's knock, and I was anxious to see him. I hurried to the door, throwing it open.

"How is Gillie?"

Wayne blinked. "She's as well as can be expected." He tilted his head. "Are you doing something different with your hair, Kiddo?"

"Awk." I ripped off the wig. "Just fooling around."

"Uh, huh."

"I'm trying to find a disguise."

"What for?" He looked over his round, metal-rimmed lenses, frowning.

"It's complicated. Come in." I motioned.

He checked his watch. "I got time. It's hard to get any rest when Gillie's in jail. My mind won't turn off." His face was gray, clothes rumpled, and his hair was askew. He tugged at the band holding his mane and let his hair loose.

"Do you want tea?" I asked as he entered. "It is a chamomile blend. Shouldn't keep you awake." I knew Wayne belonged to Alcoholics Anonymous. He had had battles with alcohol and possibly drugs when he was younger. He was proud he had kicked his disease, and I was careful not to offer him beer or wine.

"Sounds good." He said and headed to the easy chair where he sat heavily. I grabbed a tea bag and filled a cup with water and placed it in the microwave.

"You look like you need a good night's sleep."

"I sure do." He nodded, the lines on his forehead tight.

"Here you go." I handed him the cup of tea, and he took a sip. The liquid appeared to calm him, and he asked, "So, a disguise?"

My conversation with Myra about meeting a psychic paled in comparison to Wayne's situation. I felt sheepish and shrugged as I explained.

"Long story, short, Myra thinks I should meet with a psychic. The woman reads in public, and I want a disguise. I know it is a little silly." I let Wayne unwind and changed the topic. "How is Gillie? Have they made any progress in her situation?"

He brightened, "She's hanging in. I think everybody needs a view into the future these days. Heck, I might want a reading, too." He took another drink.

"I'll let you know how it goes." I smiled.

"They are holding Gillie while the medical examiner goes over Walter's medical records. She should be out Friday afternoon."

"That's good, before the weekend."

"Yep. I will be glad when she's home."

"So that means it's done?"

"Nope. It means they couldn't find enough to charge her with. They can keep investigating."

"They'd have no reason to continue." I was confident.

"That Clark woman is determined. She wants to make a name for herself." Wayne's face was grim, and he took another sip of tea. He rested the mug on the chair arm and grimaced.

"Good grief." I only met her briefly when she returned the spare keys. Along with that short visit and after viewing her professional photo at the police station, I agreed that Morgan Clark was a woman to be reckoned with.

"But there's nothing to find."

"Hope not." He shifted in the chair and looked at the mug, grimacing.

I flinched and studied him. "Is there something more?"

"They rarely test for this poison. It doesn't show up in a regular autopsy. Gillie supposedly confessed to poison. To rule that out, they have to test more samples."

"What if they don't have those?" I frowned. Walter had been deceased and buried for several years.

"Like I thought, they could dig up Walter."

"No!"

Wayne was quiet, and he gazed off into space.

"That's not going to happen. They can't," I said, shaking my head. "Gillie knows her plants, right?"

"Sure does."

"She would know if a plant was toxic?"

"Yep."

"And she wouldn't accidentally confuse one with another?"

"Anything is possible. But that don't seem like Gillie." Abruptly, he downed his tea, and said, "I'd better go." He stood and handed me his empty cup.

"If there's anything I can do, let me know." I gave Wayne a quick hug as he left. The words seemed like an empty gesture. What could I do?

I Googled the poison that Monkshood contained, stymied by our conversation. There had to be a way out of this nightmare. He had been right on. It was not a substance that they usually tested for, and Gillie knew her plants. Our best hope for Gillie was that the prosecutor dropped the investigation and left Walter in peace.

Chapter 12

The next morning, I headed over to the rehab and started the day's work. I had a week to finish clearing out the house. Retouching the paint from scuff marks left from the search could wait until after the new carpet was installed. I was eager to evaluate the lawn after the winter. Most of the snow had melted, and patches of green grass had started. I was happy to embrace the new season.

While I worked, thoughts of Wayne and Gillie's dilemma, Morgan Clark, and getting the house on the market in time for summer buyers ran through my mind. It was a little late in March to market. But April looked promising. My phone rang while I was wrapping up the prep work for painting.

It was Myra, with cool precision, "I set up the readings for Saturday afternoon with Gabriella. Will that work?"

"It will, but I do not have a clue about a disguise. My Halloween wig, well, looks pretty fake."

"Not to worry. Come over Saturday morning, and we will figure it out. I have a few wigs, and we can experiment with make-up. We'll have a snack before the readings. They are a half-hour each, and we can get lunch afterwards."

"That sounds like a blast, Myra. I can hardly wait." Myra has a few wigs. Who knew?

Humming along to "Don't Think I Don't Think About It" by Darius Rucker, I considered Gillie's homecoming on Saturday. I was deep in my thoughts when Don called.

"How about dinner?" His voice warmed me, and I felt a flush.

"Friday night is open. Saturday, I have plans with Myra."

"Glad you could fit me in." He sounded testy, and I felt a pang of guilt.

"Sorry. The plans came up fast." We usually reserved the weekends for each other. "Sunday is free too."

"All right. I can do that. Friday?"

"How about casual? Like, a pizza at my place?" I asked.

"Sounds like a great idea. Seven at your place? I'll pick up a garbage special."

"With half Hawaiian?" Canadian bacon and pineapple rocked pizza flavors for me.

"If you insist." He chuckled.

"I do. Please." In the back of my mind, it would be an opportunity to find out information on the prosecutor or Morgan Clark, and possibly get the latest on Gillie's predicament. We could talk about wedding plans. My stomach flitted at the thought.

I finished out the day, filling the dumpster with odds and ends left behind. Satisfied I was making progress, I walked around the lot, listing what spring projects needed to be done. I was at the mailbox, noted its condition, and added a new box and new house numbers to the list.

"Hello? It's Katelyn, right? You are the new owner?" The stout, middle-aged woman bellowed from the mailbox next door, where she collected her mail and paper.

"My name is Dorothy. People call me Dottie," she yelled as she trekked from her box to mine. She carried a vinyl tote, straps slung over her shoulder, in which she had stuffed her mail and shopper.

"Hello again, Dottie, and yes." I answered, looking at my notes and opening the box to check for any random flyers. "I'm fixing it up to put on the market." I resigned myself to a lengthy conversation since I had put off the chatty woman twice before.

"So, you won't live here?" The disappointment was evident in her voice.

"No." Leaving the mailbox open, I shrugged. "I own a townhome nearby."

"Well," she sighed. "That's probably better, anyway."

"Why do you say that?" Puzzled at her tone, I tilted my head.

"I don't want to gossip, mind you." She walked over and halted about two feet away. Her voice lowered. "There's been some funny goings on at this house." She peered through thick eyeglass lenses mounted into blue plastic frames.

"How so?" I closed the box and studied her.

"Well, you know the man who owned it before you is suspected of killing a man from his work?"

"Yes." I nodded, curious. "He's a person of interest."

"Well," her voice hushed. "I think he did it. And I think he killed the guy right here, in this house."

"The police searched the place and didn't find anything suspicious," I countered.

"Then why does he keep driving by?" She adjusted the straps of her carryall. "Got a bum arm," she said at my glance to the bag.

"He does?" My stomach dipped, and I felt a chill.

"It looks like that same blue van that was here into all hours of the night. I swear he loaded a body." Her voice fell to a whisper. "It was the middle of the night, and his wife, Penelope, they called her Penny, had gone to visit her mother. She is such a nice woman." She smiled. "We would talk about her jobs and how hard it was to get a full-time job as an art teacher. She filled in as a receptionist through a temp agency because of the economy and all that."

"What did you see the night you think something funny happened?"

"Just what I said. He backed into the garage, which was odd, because you only do that when you want to load or leave items. The next thing we hear is that there is a murder, and he's a suspect." She clucked. "The nerve of some people!"

"So, you didn't actually see anything?" I asked, noting her thick glasses, her eyes large behind the lenses.

"Well, no," she sounded wounded. "I told the police, though."

"So, they interviewed you?" I scanned her face, which showed the lines of a long life, but was open as she recounted her story.

"Came out for a smoke, don't sleep as well as I used to. Guess it's just age catching up." She paused, her mouth pressed, and she squinted. "What was strange, was that in all the time they lived here, lights were out early. Can't remember a time when they were on in the middle of the night. And this was two o'clock in the morning!"

"Uh, huh." I prompted her.

"Then the next thing I hear, Maxim's cleared out the tech area, and the house is for sale. They are moving way the heck south, to Minnetonka. He is getting away with murder." Her voice was harsh. "I just know it!"

"Hum. I hope that isn't the case. That won't help sell it," I kidded. "Seriously, the investigators tore up the inside looking for evidence of the crime and found nothing. It is a great house. Perfect for a family."

"Well, isn't that the funniest thing? Why would he keep driving by? He slows, looks like he is going to stop, then keeps driving."

"Are you sure it's him, or the same van?"

"As sure as I stand here. I know what I see. I see distances clearly, not so good in the reading department. But his vehicle has a broken taillight. Happened when he hit the side of the garage, when she moved in before the murder. Did not hurt the garage, but it took out the taillight." She chuckled. "She and I would talk. He wasn't as friendly."

"Sean said his wife didn't like his house. That is why they bought another one," I said.

"Yeah. He was particular, didn't want her to make any changes. Made it clear that the place was his. Set in his ways. Can't see how she was gonna live with a fella like that in any house." Her voice dropped. "It was him that was here that day while you were inside, wasn't it?"

"When?" I cocked my head, thinking back.

"The garage door went up, and it looked like he opened it? He got out of his van, looked like he had a clicker. I was checking that new bush. The winter weather killed a miniature rose bush. I should have known better. Roses are finicky."

I blinked at her account, then it registered.

"Oh yeah, he returned a garage door opener they had forgotten at closing. Scared the willies out of me." I chuckled.

"Uh huh," she clucked. Satisfied she had made her point. Sean was surveilling the house.

"He and that Arthur fellow were buddy-buddy. And there was another man that hung out with them." She cocked her head and gushed, "He was a looker, that guy. Blond, drove a red sports car." Her face flushed.

"They were quite the threesome. They played on a softball team for Maxim's."

"Really? Do you remember the blond fellow's name?"

"Let me think. There was Sean, dark hair, short buzz cut, Arthur, he was no looker, but I heard he had money. And Nathan." Her face lit up when she remembered all of them. "I always thought Nathan and Penelope would make a striking couple."

My cell phone rang, and I wished Dottie a good day and walked back to the rehab, uneasy about what she had said about Sean being set in his ways. The caller hung up before I could answer. CID said it was Eddy. I shrugged and slipped the phone back into my pocket. Eddy would leave a message if he had to talk to me.

I entered the house, mulling over Dottie's conversation. If it was Sean driving past the residence, what could he want? I opened the overhead door and examined each side. There was a small dent at the height of a vehicle to the left of the door. The paint was flaked, but nothing screamed major repair. These days, if a vehicle touched anything, it dented. Dottie's story appeared to be correct.

Chapter 13

Don knocked at my door Friday night at seven sharp. I gave one last swipe of lip gloss and ran a brush through my hair. The country music channel played in the background. I turned the music down and, breathless, answered the door, eagerly relieving him of the pizza box. His brows raised, he said, "You're welcome" to my pizza grab and stood in the doorway.

"Sorry," I kissed him on the cheek. "Come in! I am famished." Boots also eagerly sniffed the air. I gave him a stern, "You've had your dinner!" Not at all chastened, he head butted my leg as I put out the pizza, plates, and beer. I mollified him with a treat from the jar I kept on the counter.

Don slipped off his jacket and sat down at the table, and for a few minutes all was quiet except for us savoring the food. Once sated, he asked, "So, how is the rehab going?"

"It's moving along," I nodded as I snagged another slice of Hawaiian. "I met a neighbor, Dorothy. Her nickname is Dottie."

"She's the woman who lives in the rambler next door?"

"Yes. Good memory," I said. "You've met her?"

"She's memorable," he said wryly. "Yes. She calls the station, asks a lot of questions. When will the streets be swept? What is the curfew for kids? Stuff like that."

"Huh." I looked at him quizzically. "She thinks Sean backed his van up to the garage one night with the express purpose of removing a dead body," I said.

"Uh, huh." He snorted and gulped his beer.

"I told her the investigators combed the house and didn't come up with anything that points to Sean."

"But she isn't convinced." He finished my sentence.

"No. She said he drives past the house, and she finds that suspicious."

He sat back, his eyes locked with mine. My stomach did a flip-flop with the deep blue gaze. "I'll talk to her."

"She didn't tell the investigators?" I asked.

"Can't talk about an open investigation." He put his beer down and said, "Katelyn, I want you to stay with me until this job is done."

"But they didn't find anything?" I stared him down.

"Please. Humor me."

That didn't answer my question. I studied him, thinking about everything I would have to do to live in his world, and countered, "Stay here with me and Boots." Hiding my squeamishness about sharing my space, adding, "You can stay in the spare room."

"How about we trade off? One week, I stay here, the next week, you and Boots stay with me," he suggested.

"Hum. I guess that would be fair." I tapped my bottle against his. "Starting Sunday," I said, thinking of my plans with Myra. "Who goes first?"

"Why don't you and Boots come to my house? I'll have my housekeeper set up a suite for the both of you?" He cleared his throat.

I batted my lashes and blinked, and he grinned. "It'll give us more time together to plan for the wedding."

"Of course, the wedding." It came out in a squeak. I got up and started clearing the table, putting plates in the dishwasher and the leftovers in the fridge. He rose and ambled to the sink where I busied myself in the tight galley-style kitchen. In the background, the music station started a Josh Turner tune, "Why Don't We Just Dance."

"Don't be scared." His voice was low, and he placed his hands on my shoulders and turned me around to face him. Closing my eyes, I melted into his embrace as we slowly danced to the crooner.

Chapter 14

Saturday morning, I drove up Myra's winding driveway to her estate facing the 'couple's lake' in Minneapolis, where we would get into disguise prior to meeting Gabriella.

"You look happy," she commented as she opened the door.

"Don came over last night and we made plans." I grinned, still blissful from our evening.

"Good." She waved me to the kitchen and poured a steaming cup of coffee and placed it on the table at my usual chair. I took in the peaceful view of the lake from her breakfast table while she served freshly made muffins. She prompted, "Tell me." And sat in anticipation.

"We'll trade off living at each other's home until this renovation is done."

"Huh." She frowned. "That doesn't sound like a wedding plan."

"Well. No. It's a start." I mumbled. I took a muffin from the plate. "Ooh, these look good. Banana nut?"

"Harrumph." She was not buying my diversionary tactic. She must have read the panic on my face because she smiled and said, "Let's get our disguises together for the readings. We can chat later."

"Perfect." I said and put my muffin aside.

"Bring your coffee. We will try clothes and wigs upstairs."

"Sure." Myra's home was gracious and warm. Wood flooring and a spacious kitchen facing the lake spelled serenity at the highest. We grabbed our mugs, and I followed her up the staircase to an owner's suite that was half the size of the upstairs. On her dresser with the triple mirror were wig stands bearing a brown, a red, and a blonde wig.

"Pick one," she said.

"Awesome. I'll go blonde." I slipped on the wig, stuffing my unruly locks under the cap. "Is this real hair?"

"Close, it is a mix. I will go red." She adjusted the faux hair and smiled.

"Myra, that's fantastic." I stood back and watched, transfixed. "I would never know it was you. It's a fabulous disguise."

"Blonde suits you, too." She smiled. "Now, I think we can find a jacket or coat and scarf that will pass anyone's scrutiny." She dug through her closet, a spacious walk-in with a full-length Cheval mirror. "Here, try this." She pulled out a beige trench coat.

"Maybe it looks a little too obvious? All I need is a pair of big sunglasses and I could pass for a spy?" I squinted at my reflection. "Wasn't there an actress that wore a coat like this?"

"There were several who did." She laughed and pulled out a casual navy-blue jacket. "This is more subtle." I slipped it on over my cream-colored shirt.

"Looks good." I stood in front of the mirror and twirled, checking the back. "Yep. This is it." The change from dark, unkempt locks to a cool bob hairstyle made me look hip, polished. "I could go blonde."

"That's good," she said. "It looks natural."

"Do you do this often?" I asked. I was beginning to wonder about the different wigs. Did Myra have a secret life I wasn't privy to? We all have secrets, but the woman I knew was a straight arrow, cultured, conservative, steady rock I could depend on. This made me curious.

"No." She sent me a look that said, 'no more questions.' She slipped on a tan jacket and coordinated scarf. With the red wig, she was striking. We struck a pose together in front of the mirror, then I snapped a cell phone selfie for fun.

"This is great," I chortled. "Let's do it!" We trooped downstairs, grabbed our handbags, and went to Myra's SUV.

Chapter 15

After parking in front of the massive Victorian on the main drag of Hiptown, we checked our disguises, snickered, and with firm resolve stalked to the door. I gave the door knocker a brisk thump, and a woman threw open the door.

"Hello. I am Gabriella!" She spoke English with a slight accent, and she was six feet tall. A big woman with long, dark hair curling around her bosom. She wore a silky, caftan-like garment that covered her heft and waved us in with long nails painted a deep red. Hushed at her imposing presence, we mutely followed her direction.

"Who wants reading first?" she asked in her broken dialect. Myra and I looked at one another. "I do one at a time. Not together. Will disturb one person's aura if reading together."

"You go first, Myra." I smiled and claimed a chair in the entry. A peek inside the adjoining room confirmed it was the reading room with a crystal ball set on a round table covered with a red velvet cloth.

"All right." Myra clenched her jaw and gave me a cool glance as she preceded Gabriella into the room. I feigned an innocent 'who me' look. I heard the murmur of voices while seated outside the door. Studying the sign posted on the door Gabriella had ushered Myra through, I considered my options. Her readings were listed, and it was intriguing, one or both palms, tarot cards, and psychic or medium. Gabriella had to be talented to pull off the variety. I settled on a palm reading and looked around for any other reading material. Finding none, I fidgeted, crossing and uncrossing my legs.

Finally, I stood and peered out of the side windows of the front door that faced the busy street and gazed longingly at the pizza parlor across the street. My mouth watered at the idea of a sweet and spicey Hawaiian pizza. While I scanned the street lunch crowd, my breath quickened at the sight of a familiar sheriff's car parked at the curb in front of the pizza place. Don got out along with a stout, blonde, woman in uniform.

"Ah, the ambitious Morgan Clark," I muttered. "But man cannot live by pizza alone," I added, thinking of our blissful evening, and remembering the warmth of Don's arms around me as we danced to the music.

"Thank you." Myra's muffled voice came. The door opened and Gabriella remained seated at the small table inside the reading room. Myra smiled tightly. "Your turn." Her complexion had paled, and the red wig emphasized the contrast.

"Are you all right?" I asked in a low tone. She gave a sharp nod and sat in the chair I had occupied. "You look like you might be sick."

"No. Go. She's waiting." Her voice matched my whisper.

"Okay." I was uncertain. "If you want a giggle, watch for Don and his detective at lunch across the street." She smiled, and color returned to her complexion. "I may do that."

I entered the small room and sat across from Gabriella, who opened her eyes and appeared to come out of a trance.

"What do you want today?" She asked in a monotone.

"A palm reading." My throat was scratchy, and I cleared the cough that threatened.

"One or both palms?" she asked.

"Just one today."

"You are right-handed?"

"Yes."

"I will read that palm. It is the dominant one." She reached for my hand and enveloped it with her own large mitts. She flipped it to the palm side, and her breath caught. I tensed as she peered, then traced the lines with one long nail. "There is trouble."

"What trouble?" I frowned. My limited knowledge of fortune tellers and psychics said they weren't supposed to give scary predictions. It was entertainment, with a peek into the future. Maybe help sort out the funk in someone's mind. Didn't this woman know that?

"You cannot dance with only one man!" My breath came in short spurts and my hand trembled. I felt my face go warm. "There are many loves! Ah, at least two!"

"There is danger in your money line!" She sat back and looked up at the ceiling with a dramatic sigh. I withdrew my hand from where she held it between her cool ones and shivered.

"Okay. That's good." My legs were shaky as I rose. I dug money from my purse and left it on the table. She sent me a harsh gaze through half-closed eyes with a slight nod toward a sign that read "Tips Appreciated." I ignored the sign and made my escape.

Myra waited in the foyer, clutching her handbag, her color ashen. Through gritted teeth, I demanded. "Let's go!"

Don and his deputy were outside the restaurant as Myra started her car. About to enter his vehicle, he stopped, startled, and stared at Myra's SUV, as she gunned the engine and drove off in the opposite direction. Out of sight from the sheriff, Myra ripped off her wig and tossed it in the back seat.

"What a quack!" she grumbled. "Wait until I talk to Bernie."

"What did she say to you?"

"Let's find a lunch place first." She drove to a deli style café, where we ordered at the counter, picked up our food, and found a cushy booth. The colors of the interior were bright and welcoming, and the pastries were to die for. Mindful of the carbs after the earlier muffin, I shrugged and tore off a piece of the rich caramel roll, thinking this was almost as good as the pizza I had craved.

The stress of Gabriella's reading faded with each bite of the roll. I asked, "So, what did she say?" Myra had fluffed her hair from the confines of the wig. Her color had returned, and she regained her calm nature. I had kept my hairpiece on, glancing occasionally into a window to see my reflection. The faux hair behaved, keeping its style, unlike my natural hair, and I was rather hooked on my image as a blonde.

"She said I couldn't dance with just one man." She said wryly, sniffing. "Too many men. I am good at being on my own and intend to stay that way."

"No way! She told me the same thing!" I inhaled. "And I'm engaged." My fingers brushed over the solitaire diamond.

"Really?" Myra frowned. "Then she gave a warning about danger with money."

"Same here. She is a fraud!" Shaking my head, "I can't believe she gave us the same reading."

"I will talk to Bernie." She pursed her lips, and a snicker escaped. "How did you like her enormous sigh, and looking to the heavens schtick?"

"OMG and then she wanted a tip!" I choked on a bit of roll, which led to a coughing fit. Tears ran down my cheeks, and I wiped them away. "Of course, she cursed me because I didn't tip."

"We can cross Gabriella off our list," Myra said, and chuckled.

Calmer, I mused, "I thought it odd that she used the word 'dance'."

She shrugged and gazed at me. "Could mean anything. Why?"

"Um, nothing." I polished off my pastry. Maybe I took it too literally, but my dance with Don the night before was a sweet memory, mingled with a case of nerves. "So, did you get a look at Morgan Clark?"

"No. I was too busy making a getaway. The nerve of that fraud!" She shook her head. "How is Gillie?"

"Not sure. Wayne said they were holding her for 48 hours, and then if there wasn't enough to charge her, they would let her go. She should be out by now."

"If they don't have anything," Myra said, raising her brows.

"They won't. They can't?" Shaking my head, I said, "Gillie would not hurt a fly. I'll call." I dug out my phone and hit Wayne's contact number. It went to voice mail. "They are likely unwinding from Gillie's release. I don't want to bother them." I tucked the phone in my bag.

"How's the rehab going?" she asked.

"I'm making progress. After the carpet installers on Thursday, it is nearly finished. After the carpet is in, I will touch up the scuff marks. It is a shame the investigators tore up the place. It may have been sold by now."

"Did they ever find anything?" she asked. Myra finished her croissant and gazed at me.

"You know the drill. Cannot comment on an ongoing investigation, per you-know-who." I shrugged.

"Yes. That would be Sheriff Don Williams, your husband-to-be." She lifted her cup in a mock toast and a twinkle in her eyes. "Any new wedding plans?" She put her cup down and sat back. I felt her gaze as my face reddened. I knew Myra wanted me to be happy, but I needed to sort out my nerves about getting married.

Squelching my case of jitters, I said, "Um, no. Just trading weeks, staying at each other's places while I finish this rehab."

"Is there something else going on with the rehab?" She brushed the front of her coat and shifted, tilting her head.

Relieved at the change of subject, "I met a neighbor at the mailbox this past week, and she says she has seen Sean's blue van driving past. He slows down as if he is going to stop at the house, then drives past."

"She thinks it's Sean Young?"

"Yes. She is sure it's him because the van's taillight is broken." I gulped. "She claims she knows which night he removed a body."

"Of the dead co-worker?" She blinked.

"Yes." I nodded. "She couldn't sleep, so she went outside to smoke. The van backed into the garage, and she thinks that's when Sean took out the body."

"She thinks the murder happened inside the house?"

"Guess so." I met her gaze. "Sean claims the blood in the house was his. He stepped on broken glass; he is a hemophiliac, and the gun I found did not belong to him."

Myra shook her head. "But if it's him driving by, he must be looking for something?"

"I guess. That's why Don wants me and Boots to stay with him. It would be fairer if we traded off weekends."

"Relationships are all about compromise." She chuckled.

My cell sounded, and I plucked it out of my bag. "It's Wayne!"

"Hey Kiddo. I saw you called. Just thought you'd want to know, Gillie's home."

"That is great, Wayne. How is she?" I looked over at Myra and gave her a thumbs up.

"She's a mite tired. Doesn't understand all this blathering about getting DNA or digging up Walter."

"Well, they want to be sure it wasn't the plant that killed him. They must test for the poison."

"She's got a memory box. Has his shaving brush and hairbrush, and she took a lock of his hair before they buried him."

"Wayne, that is terrific! They can test hair." I frowned. "What do you mean, a shaving brush?"

"It's one of those old-time brushes that men used to lather their face with shaving cream. Don't see a lot of that anymore." He chuckled.

"That sounds like a done deal for testing. They shouldn't need anything more."

"Hope not."

I hung up, relieved, and sat back.

"Gillie's out. She has got a memory box."

"A what?" Myra's nose wrinkled.

"Wayne called it a memory box. She kept personal items from Walter. Shaving brush, hairbrush, lock of hair, that sort of thing."

"That should be perfect for testing."

"Uh huh. They won't have to dig up Walter, after all." I smiled widely, delighted at the news.

"Gillie must be sentimental," Myra mused. "I didn't keep any of that stuff from Marvin." Marvin was Myra's much beloved, now departed husband.

"I kept some things." I tilted my head, remembering Jake. It had become a blur with time, except for the jolt of pain when they told me he had died. "His ring, cards. Hair, I am kind of a mush, too." I smiled gamely.

"We both weathered storms, and it is on to brighter days." Myra smiled, trying to lift our moods.

"Yes. We should go." My stomach had done a deep dive, and I did not want to talk about getting married. For the third time.

Myra drove back to her home, and after a speedy stop at the bathroom to remove the blonde wig and tame my dark mane, I gave her a quick hug and left. I avoided more questions, but not her curious gaze.

"Talk later," I called, waving from my driver's window. Out of sight, I banished all thoughts of wedding plans and headed home.

Chapter 16

Wayne and Gillie were at the mailboxes as I drove in and parked in my garage stall. They lingered at the townhome's entrance.

"Gillie! I am so glad you are home!" I exclaimed, as I hurried to meet up with the couple.

"Me, too. I don't get why they think I'm a killer," she protested. "That Morgan gal, she had me locked up for a crime I didn't commit. It isn't fair." Her pixie hair was dyed a deep plum color, and her hoodie and sweat outfit matched her hair color. Her complexion was drawn, and fatigue lined her face.

"It was 'cuz you confessed, honey," Wayne said.

"How can I be held responsible for what I say when I am fast asleep?" she protested. "That Clark woman had no business locking me up," she declared.

"Calm down, honey. They have got the memory box, and they can test for the poison. It'll be over soon."

"All they had to do is ask. They didn't have to lock me up," she muttered.

"I'm sorry you went through that, Gillie," I said.

"Gretta. You have got to call me Gretta!" she spouted. "You keep calling me Gillie, 'cuz of Walter, the husband I supposedly killed."

"It's Gretta from now on," I promised. "It will all work out. It's a big mistake." The woman was stressed, and I regretted calling her Gillie, a form of Gilman, her former last name, which Wayne and I both used. She and Wayne were married now, but the nickname had stuck.

"No need for your feathers to be ruffled, honey." Wayne put his arm around her shoulder. "You need to get some sleep." He led her to their unit, and I headed to mine.

"It's good to have you home, Gretta," I said. This was going to be a challenge. I should have known the nickname would bother her. It was like Eddy calling me "Wifey." We had sparred over that until he'd dropped that in favor of Kate or Katie. I hurried inside, preoccupied with the thought of packing out for a week at Don's house. Boots pounced at my legs.

"Okay, treats, it is." I gave Boots a tidbit and sunk into the sofa, exhausted from the afternoon.

Rat-a-tat. I answered the door, puzzled at Wayne's knock so soon.

"Don't pay no mind to Gil... 'er Gretta. She's tired and cranky with all that's going on," he said in a hushed tone. He was weary, but looked relieved as he stood in the hall outside my door.

"No problem." I shook my head. "You've both been through the wringer these days. They have the items to test, right?"

"Yep. It'll be a while, could be as long as a month or two. We'll stick around until we get the results." He shrugged.

"So no get away for the two of you?" I asked.

"Nope. Figure it's better if we keep our routine. If you need help at the rehab, just let me know."

"Are you sure?"

"Yep. If I hang around too much, we'll just get in each other's hair." He chuckled. "We already got one guy's hair being tested." Wayne had a gallows humor that took getting used to.

"I am having carpet layers in on Thursday. It would be great if I could have the mantel finished before they come?"

"I'll be there first thing Monday." He turned to leave.

"Perfect! Oh, and Wayne? I'm taking Boots tomorrow and we are going to stay at Don's place this coming week. I'll stop in here and there, but we'll be gone at night. That is the plan, anyway. Don will stay here the following week." I shrugged.

"It sure gets complicated, don't it?" He winked.

"It does." I nodded.

"Thanks for letting me know. I would have worried." He nodded.

"I'll see you Monday at the rehab." Smiling, I shut the door and went to join Boots on the sofa for a nap. I closed my eyes, then heard another knock. "What the heck?"

I peered out the security hole. Eddy. Frowning, I opened the door. If Eddy saw my dismay, he didn't show it. He brushed past.

"Hey Katie, am I glad to see you!" He dropped onto the sofa, and Boots head butted him for a pet. He stroked the cat's fur and grinned.

Slowly, I closed the door and asked, "What's up, Eddy?" Crossing my arms, my head cocked, I stared at him.

"Well, Katie, you won't believe this, but Lola kicked me out."

My eyes narrowed, and I retorted, "She can't kick you out. You are on the lease agreement."

"Lola's a force, Katie. Kind of like you," he said.

"What did you do?" I asked, my gaze steady.

"Got canned!" He stretched out on the sofa and flung one gangly arm over his eyes. It was déjà vu, Eddy on my sofa, unemployed.

"For what?" I snapped.

"Didn't show for a meeting after my shift. I fell asleep. They said it was mandatory. After the fact." His body heaved a sigh.

"Isn't that like a write-up or a verbal warning?"

"I was on probation."

"Probation?" I frowned.

"When they stuck me on nights, they started a probationary period."

"Yee gads, Eddy. You cannot be doing this. You are wasting your life, grow up."

"Yeah, I know, I screwed up. I'll get another job."

He always did. Sometimes it didn't pay as well. But eventually he landed an employer. It wouldn't help to lecture.

"I'll put on the coffee." And I headed to the kitchen.

"Thanks Katie." He called, "Can I stay here until I find a job?" My head dropped. I stood at the kitchen sink, running water for the coffee. Rearing up, I yelled, "No! Why can't you stay in your own house?" He had signed the rental agreement for my Bluebird flip, not Lola.

"Lola said I couldn't come back until I had a job," he whined.

Lola had more sense than I did. Good for her. But somebody has to pay the rent.

"You have a spare room. I wouldn't get in the way. You would hardly know I was here."

"Eddy, I'm making big changes here." I returned and sat in the easy chair, facing him. "I am engaged to be married. You and Lola must work this out." He closed his eyes and groaned. I studied his face. He had a shadow of a beard, and his dark hair was mussed, which made his dare devil good looks more appealing. I steeled myself against turning to mush. Hearing the last drip of the coffeemaker, I brought us each a mug. He swung his legs over the edge of the sofa and took the cup.

"She'll change the locks," he grumbled.

"I don't think she will. She is probably mad because she has to carry the load, pay the rent for a house she isn't on the contract for. If she wants to stay there." Once upon a time, I had been there with Eddy, too.

He gulped his java.

"Okay, Katie. I'll try. Can I stay here tonight until she cools down? Please? Pretty please?"

Boots added a pleading 'meow' to Eddy's whine.

"All right. But just for tonight. I have plans for tomorrow and the coming weeks. I have a house to rehab, and Don and I have plans."

"Like what?" His dark eyes sparkled, and color returned to his face.

"I'll spend this coming week at his house, and he's going to stay here the week following." I was reluctant to divulge my agreement with Don to Eddy, but here he was.

"What about Boots?" he asked.

"He's coming with."

"So, your place will be empty, anyway? That's harsh, Katie." Yeah, I knew it was too much information.

"I will be in and out. Besides, you and Lola have to resolve your problems," I said firmly.

"You're living the life, Katie. He has great digs." Eddy grinned.

I bit my lip to keep from giving another lecture about compatibility and merging lives, and said, "Yes Eddy, he has an awesome place." Don's home was nestled in an upscale area of private homes with acreage. It stood in stark contrast to my two-bedroom, two-bath, cozy townhome.

The problem with Don that niggled at me was that he never told me he was wealthy. I had not pried when he hadn't offered his place until well into our relationship. Then it came as a shock. I reeled from the knowledge, even as I accepted his proposal. By now, the news had settled in, and I was becoming more comfortable with his money, although puzzled why he wouldn't have disclosed it sooner. I put it down to men are just plain weird sometimes. Like now, with Eddy.

"So, you're packing out for his place tomorrow?" Eddy asked.

"I should pack tonight. Be ready to leave in the morning with Boots, and head over."

"That should be entertaining." He snorted. "Boots likes his home."

"Yes, he does." Boots sprawled on the back of the sofa, watching our conversation. Occasionally, Eddy reached back to scratch him, and he accepted the strokes contentedly.

"So, we have tonight?"

"Where are you going with this, Eddy?"

"We could go to Ivan's, have a bite, watch the band?" he asked. "My treat?"

"You should keep your money. Right now, you're homeless."

"You were always so practical, Kate."

"Uh, huh."

"Well," he stood up, "I'll get my things from the truck."

"Things, you have things?" I sputtered.

"Yeah, Lola threw some stuff into a suitcase." He headed to the exit. "I'll get it."

"It's just for one night, Eddy," I warned him. His long legs were out the door and down the hall, and out to his truck.

I leaned back in the easy chair and closed my eyes. Boots hopped from the sofa and wound his body around my legs, meowing. "You want food, right?" I stroked the cat until Eddy burst back into the room with the suitcase. I blinked at the sight of a large, gray luggage case.

"That's not an overnight suitcase."

"I'll be back." He wheeled the bag to the spare room. I got up and followed. He threw the case on the bed and grinned. "I'll unpack later. Any beer?"

"No unpacking, Eddy." I rubbed my temple and headed back to the living room. "Just take out what you need. Leave the suitcase packed. No beer."

"No beer," he echoed, following me. "Okie doke." He shrugged, "Any snacks?"

"Leftover pizza. In the fridge, help yourself." I returned to the living room with shoulders slumped, rubbed my temple, and gripped my coffee mug.

"Great!" he brightened, snagged a piece of cold pizza, and commandeered the sofa.

"How's Gillie?" he asked.

I caught him up to speed on my neighbor's dilemma, ending with, "Be sure to call her Gretta if you see her."

My phone rang, interrupting my account, and noting the CID, I said, "Have to take this." I snatched up the receiver and headed to my bedroom for privacy.

"Hello, Don?" I was happy, but nervous about talking to Don with Eddy in the next room.

"Hey, it's Saturday night. Why don't I stop over and help you collect Boots, and we can grab dinner somewhere and get you settled over here tonight?"

"No! I mean, I haven't packed yet, and Myra and I had a huge lunch, so I'm not very hungry. We should stick to the original plan. I will drive over, say, mid-morning. We can do brunch." I hoped he wouldn't hear the panic in my voice. Not that I couldn't tell him about Eddy. I just wanted Eddy gone before I left for his house.

"Well, sure. If that's what you want to do." He sounded wary.

"It is. I'm sorry but I have to go. Boots is yowling again." I chuckled nervously. In the background, the cat was loudly protesting in the kitchen at the treat jar.

"I will see you in the morning. Sleep tight." His low voice came. "Miss you."

"Me, too," and I hung up, my stomach churning about the deception. I headed to the kitchen and scooted the cat off the counter. "No more treats."

Feeling guilty about not being entirely truthful with Don, I surveyed Eddy lounging on the sofa. He gave me a knowing smile.

"Trouble in paradise, Katie?"

"You have to be out by eight o'clock tomorrow morning. I have to pack now."

"No problem." He studied me through narrowed eyes that hinted at mirth. I turned toward the bedroom.

"How's the latest project going?" he asked.

"A nosy neighbor says the former owner, Sean, does drive-by's at night." I faced him.

"Really?" He sat up straight. "What's that about?"

"Don't know. Don wants me to stay with him until this house is done. He doesn't like the sound of it and thinks I would be safer there."

"Good man. I agree." He nodded.

"Thanks Eddy." My heart warmed that he cared about my safety. It was the first positive thing I had heard him say about Don that I could recall. "Good night." And I left for the bedroom.

"'Night Kate."

Chapter 17

When I awoke Sunday morning, Eddy was gone and had left a note, "Thanks, Katie. You are the best!" and he had signed with a smiley face. Relieved he had kept his word, I sprang into action, got Boots' carrier out and finished packing. One overnight case with the essentials and a change of clothes. I could return to the townhouse for anything more. My nerves were a jumble as I loaded Boots into the crate and motored over to Don's place. He met me at the circular driveway in front of his palatial home. Esther, his housekeeper, stood inside the entry, with a broad smile, holding the door open. She wore a blue dress, a white cardigan, and sensible white sneakers. I understood her attire as her work uniform. It seemed formal, and I had asked her about it.

"This is how I separate my work clothes from my fun clothes," she laughed. "Mr. Williams doesn't care, but I don't want to wreck my play clothes." She winked. I chuckled in agreement; my work uniform was a sweatshirt and jeans.

"Let's unload here," Don greeted me, his eyes lit up. He wore a comfortable blue plaid flannel shirt that complemented the very blue hue of his gaze.

"Sure." I got out and removed the overnight case from the back of my Ford Escape and lifted out Boots' carrier. He hissed, his back hunched, plastered against the rear of the carrier.

Don grabbed the small case. "That's all?" He looked bewildered. He left the suitcase with Esther.

"I can stop at home if needed," I said, and grabbed Boots' carrier. He was vocal, howling his displeasure at being taken from his normal environment. Over the yowling, Don called, "I'll park your car in the garage. Esther will show you to your room."

"Welcome!" Esther smiled, and I followed, struck mute by the overwhelming grandeur of the home. "Your kitty is not happy."

I had stuffed a few of Boots' treats in the pocket of my jean jacket and tried to bribe him with a snack. He yowled louder. Esther waved me ahead of her into a bedroom, and I had a glimpse of the spacious room before I dug into my messenger bag for a catnip mouse and slipped it into his cage. Boots emitted a grunt and grudgingly batted the mouse.

"He likes that." Esther smiled. "Good kitty." She placed the suitcase on a padded bench at the foot of the bed.

"Yes, he does." Placing the cage on the floor, I gazed around the room. "This is beautiful." Long drapes framed a vast window. Looking out, I was treated by an expansive view of the lake. Ripples coursed through the water and gave off an aura of serenity. I pivoted to my right and peered into a massive bathroom with a soaking tub, vanity, and separate shower. The tension from the drive on the rough and ready 35W freeway eased. The tranquility of the room revived me.

"Mr. Williams has the suite next door," she said.

"Yes. He does." Don appeared at the doorway. "Thank you, Esther." She left.

"I think you'll be comfortable here." Boots gave a wail. "It may take a while for Boots." He nodded toward the cat, who had dropped the catnip toy and stared out. "It's just me, Boots." He kneeled and reached inside the carrier to stroke his fur. Boots wasn't having it and moved to the farthest point of the carrier and glared. His tail swished.

I opened his carrier, and he stayed at the back.

"I'll leave the carrier open for now. If he has a treat and the catnip, he will settle down and feel safe enough to roam about the room," I said. "This is a lot for him. He is used to having the run of the townhouse."

"Whatever you think. I want you both to be comfortable here. Let's leave him be for now, and I will reacquaint you with the place." He smiled. This would be my first time staying in his domain. We had fallen into the habit of hanging out at my place, going to Ivan's for quiet dinners, and dancing on the weekends. Movies at the local theater or walks in Crocus Heights and window shopping in the sleepy downtown.

"I'll fill his water dish." I hurried from the bathroom sink with the bowl and placed it in the carrier. Straightening up, I brushed back my hair. He leaned in to plant a kiss on my mouth, and I inhaled. "Nice."

"Uh huh, there's more from where that came from," he murmured. Grinning, he took my hand. We walked out to the hall, and he stopped at the next room. "My room," he said. His bedroom was a matching suite to the one I would stay in. Although we were a couple, I was happy to have my space. Especially given Boots' tantrum.

"Let's grab brunch at Joseph's."

"Sure." I had been on a food fest the past few days, but Joseph's was hard to turn down.

***

We were seated at the restaurant overlooking the lake and helped ourselves to the grand buffet, which had an egg dish, pancakes, ham, sausages, and more. My mouth watered at the table filled with food. Inwardly, I counted calories, gave up, and snagged a pancake, topping it with strawberries and whipped cream.

After we took a few bites, I said, "I've been curious about Arthur Brett Cook."

"Can't talk about an ongoing investigation." He sent me a sideways glance.

"It isn't about the investigation. It is about the man," I persisted.

"What about him?" Don lifted his coffee cup to his mouth and peered over the rim.

"No one deserves to get murdered, but why do you suppose someone killed him? And over a silly promotion, no less." I watched him closely.

"People have killed for less, Katelyn." He gave a resigned smile, sipped coffee, and placed the cup on the table.

"I suppose," I mused, "But there were rumors he slept with many women? It could have been a jealous husband, or another female rival. Why do you think it was because of a job?"

"That is motive, Katelyn. They were up for the same position. Sean admitted he took work reports from his desk. He was jealous because Arthur got the job he wanted. Rumor is they were the best of friends, until Arthur got what he wanted, the promotion."

"Really?" I sipped my coffee, which, I noted, was delicious. Strong, dark, with a rich flavor. "What about the other man who was up for the same promotion? Nathan Winner?"

"It's still an ongoing investigation." He shrugged.

"Oh?" I paused, while Don went on. "Arthur was ugly and arrogant. He lusted after and got the promotion. Not that it matters. He did not deserve a bullet to the head.

"Ugly?" I laughed, snorting. "Physically ugly? Ugly is in the eye of the beholder and can be an aphrodisiac, particularly if a man has power."

"Even with a shaved head and thick black eyeglasses, he was like catnip to lonely women, usually those with the least power." He frowned.

"Hum, it must be the glasses," I teased. "And bald can be cute."

"Let's change the subject." He sat back. "I shouldn't give you my opinions of dead men." He leaned towards me; his arms rested on the table. "When and where should we get married?"

"Umm," I squeaked and lowered my coffee cup. Glancing at the buffet line, my mouth dropped open. I hunched down and said in a low voice, "Look, over there." And motioned to the food station. "Is that who I think it is?"

"What?" Bemused, he scanned the line. "Who?" He saw the man. "It's Sean Young," and he turned toward me.

"Is that his wife?" The pudgy, nondescript man was with a statuesque brunette. She wore her long hair in a flip harking back to an earlier decade, which looked fashionable with her tall, regal pose. She wore ballerina flats and had six inches on his height. Sean placed his hand on the small of her back as they left the buffet line and took a table facing the lake. He pulled out her chair before seating himself.

"Probably," Don shrugged. "It is Sunday. Many people go to brunch. Even suspected killers."

"This is a distance from Crocus Heights, or their new house." I cocked my head, "Dottie said they moved south to Minnetonka. That is at least an hour's drive."

"I will repeat. It is Sunday, Katelyn." He raised his brows, "So, you're on a first name basis with the neighbor? Dorothy Barker?"

"We aren't chummy." I winced at his change in attitude. "But people like to talk to me." I smiled. "Dottie is a talker." I batted my lashes. "It's how I solve these cases and flip houses. People talk, and I listen. And I am just a little nosy."

He chuckled at my antics, then looked serious. "Don't get too close. This guy is suspected of killing his coworker. If he can do that to a former friend, what could he do to a nosy home renovator?"

"Hum." I watched Sean and his wife discreetly. "Doesn't she look like she's out of his league?" I whispered. "She is so well put together. He is wearing a rumpled coat and looks as if he hasn't combed his hair or shaved."

"That's enough, Katelyn. We will get him if he is the murderer." He leaned in. "How about we elope?"

"To Vegas, like Wayne and Gil, 'er Gretta?"

"Perhaps somewhere more exotic," he said, and smiled.

"You know, Boots is a homebody?" I choked.

"We're not taking the cat." He sat back and stared, baffled.

"Love me, love my cat." I gazed into his deep blues and blinked.

"I love you. But I do not think a cat should be part of our nuptials."

"Boots is not just a cat." I was firm. "He's family."

He studied me for a long minute, then relented, "He can be at the wedding if we have it here. But he is not coming on our honeymoon."

"I'll think about it," I conceded with a coy smile.

"Check please!" He stood and waved over the server.

Chapter 18

The tension in the air evaporated as Don drove the scenic route past the lake homes in his sensible Buick. He had replaced the vehicle that Olivia, aka Robin Steele, had stolen with another Buick, same color, but the current year. Olivia had appeared from nowhere and had conned him, saying she was his love child. She left, taking money, credit cards, and said Buick, when he had confronted her about her nastiness toward me. His confrontation warmed me, and her thievery had done her in.

At least he had not taken the racy red Corvette on this jaunt, and the ride was relaxing. With early spring, trees and shrubs were greening up, and the lake community was coming to life, with residents putting out docks and patio furniture. Lulled by the warm air and good food, we returned to the mansion.

Esther met us at the entrance.

"Your kitty is not happy," she reported. "He is making huge noises."

"I'll take care of it." I hurried inside, with Don looking on, perplexed. Maybe I had turned into a crazy cat lady, but Boots had been with me through a lot of ups and downs. We were a team. I burst into the suite and halted, horrified. Boots had climbed the luxurious full-length drapes and had wedged his body between the wall and draperies, clinging to the top of the rod. He yowled at me as I hurried to the window.

"Boots, come down!" He stared at me.

"Come down. Right now!" More stares, and he licked his paw for emphasis. I looked around for a chair. The bathroom held a dressing table where I imagined the lady of the house could do her make-up. I snatched up the stool and placed it within reach of Boots. Balanced on the stool, I stretched up to reach him. I grabbed the cat from his perch. The stool teetered, and I crashed to the ground.

"Ouch!"

"Yowl!"

Don and Esther rushed into the room where I lay on the floor, having dropped Boots in the fall.

"Are you okay?" Don reached me first and dropped to his knees.

"Mamma Mia!" Esther exclaimed.

Boots scampered out to the hall.

"I will get your kitty," Esther said, and hurried from the room.

I sat up, and said, "My ankle hurts. I have to get Boots." I struggled to my feet with Don's arms around my waist, supporting me.

"Let's get you to the bed," he said. "Esther will corral Boots."

I moaned as I hobbled to the bed. Don sat beside me and leaned over to examine my ankle. He rubbed it. It was turning red and felt sore. I had had worse falls, so I knew all would be just fine with his warm, soft hands massaging my ankle, and with my cat back.

I heard Esther calling as she ran down the hall, "Here kitty, kitty."

After Don finished manipulating my ankle, he brushed my hair from my face, "You didn't hit your head, did you?"

"No. It knocked the air out of me," I admitted. "I'll lay down for a minute," and stretched back on the bed.

"Good idea," he said, and moved my legs onto the bed, covering me with a plush throw from the foot of the bed.

I smiled contentedly, enjoying the attention, and closed my eyes. He held my hand while I rested.

"I've got your kitty!" Esther returned, grasping the sulky cat under her arm. "He loves tuna."

"That's how I got him." I reached for Boots, who accepted a pet, then found a fluffy pillow and curled up.

"Hey, Boots. He is calmer now," Don said, and nodded.

"He looks okay. He was hungry." Esther said.

"Boots is always up for more food," I said. "I fed him earlier."

"No problem, he's good, now," Esther said.

"I'll leave you to rest, Katelyn. You are sure you don't need a doctor?" Don asked.

"No doctor," I said, and closed my eyes. They both left while Boots snoozed on the pillow next to my head.

***

Don and I shared a kiss before he left the next morning for work. My ankle was sore, but it felt stable, and I gathered Boots and headed off to the rehab. My drive from his mansion took me past the main headquarters of Maxim's, and I slowed, recalling my conversation with him about how Arthur Brett Clark had a propensity for wooing women at the company. He had preyed on the lonely and those lacking power.

Curious, I took the freeway exit that led to the imposing structure. Parking in the visitors' lot, I observed the huge glass façade that stretched up many stories and tried to imagine working with the other smartly dressed employees of the company. Sitting in my vehicle, eyes shaded by sunglasses, I watched, trying to be as inconspicuous as possible. My small gray Ford

SUV was dusty, and I was all too aware it needed a wash. The parking lot boasted clean, shiny cars, much like the people who worked there.

"No way." I breathed and slunk down into my seat, lowering the visor. A tall woman wearing large sunglasses and a trench coat, a designer purse slung over her shoulder, stepped from a vehicle and strode up to the entrance. Sun highlighted her long, dark hair. Flats had been replaced by three-inch heels and her gait was one of a model on the catwalk. "Sean's wife?" I watched her enter the building, then started my car.

I motored from the parking lot, mulling over her presence, curious why Sean wasn't with her. By the time I parked beside the roll-off dumpster in the rehab's driveway on Thrush Street, I convinced myself that it must have been a mirage. It posed the question of where Sean worked now. Had he left Maxim's under a cloud of suspicion? It would not be a good look for a corporation to have a suspected murderer in the mix. But if it was Sean Young's wife, what was she doing there? She had looked like part of the workforce, despite her regal bearing. She had not wavered in throwing open the door to the company, as a visitor might. My casual workwear had convinced me I shouldn't enter the building, and I left, vowing to return another time.

Chapter 19

Entering the renovation through the front door, I made a note to call the container company to pick up the dumpster later that day. I had brought Boots in his carrier to save Don's furnishings. He had slept through the morning but was awake now and looked annoyed that his slumber had been disturbed. After sleeping on the spacious bed, he was now relegated to his crate. I slipped him a treat and put his carrier in a corner of the family room, away from my work. He snapped up the morsel, curled up, and settled down.

After removing my diamond ring and placing it in a drawer of the powder room vanity, I got to work. There were a few items to dispose of in the basement. The downstairs area was finished with drywall and ceiling tiles. It would be a plus for sales, but the utility room remained unfinished, with a few hiccups. I considered the free-standing shelving in the furnace room and decided it could stay for the new lucky buyers-to-be.

Flipping on my trusty work radio to country music and singing along to Alan Jackson's "A Hard Hat and A Hammer," I moved the shelving aside to sweep the floor. A pair of eyeglass frames caught on one edge, and I picked them up. My hands shook when I viewed the black plastic frames, remembering Don's description of Sean's rival for the promotion. Ugly glasses and arrogant.

"Whatcha got?" Gasping, I whirled to face Wayne, and dropped the glasses.

"You scared me half to death!"

"Sorry. I rang the doorbell, but there was no answer. You still want me to work today?"

"Yes, of course. I've been so distracted by everything, Don, the rehab, Eddy, I completely forgot." Silently I cursed myself for leaving the door open in my fog.

"I hear ya." He nodded somberly. "It's been a trip."

I was instantly remorseful.

"How is Gil. . . Gretta?" I bit my tongue, correcting the slip.

"No worries." He smiled. "Waiting for the lab results on the stuff she kept. Name's a tongue twister for me, too. She's touchy about the nickname, especially now."

"Yeah. It is tough." I nodded. "Sorry. I just found this pair of glasses." I snagged the frames again and examined them. He peered over my shoulder and I offered them. He studied the remaining temple. One temple was missing and looked as if it had been twisted off at the hinge.

"Looks like a gal might wear them? There are some little stones on the temple, could be diamonds."

"Yes, that is curious. They look expensive, but most likely they're rhinestones," I said. "They could belong to Sean's wife?"

"Who's Sean?"

"The former owner."

"That guy, the one who might have killed his coworker. Do I want to know any more?" His eyes twinkled.

"Maybe not," I winced and met his gaze.

"Oh, boy." He rubbed his chin, heaving a sigh. "You sure know how to pick them."

"It wasn't my fault," I protested. "The place was a good deal, and I didn't know about the murder."

Wayne belly-laughed, stopped, and between snorts said, "So, you want me to fix the mantel?" I slipped the glasses into the pocket of my jean jacket.

"Yes. Let's take a look."

We trooped upstairs to the family room and considered the project.

"I thought I could update the fireplace with a new mantel with a thicker slab rather than the curved edges? It would give a more contemporary feel with the granite facing on the surround."

"Yep. That would work. Is that why you took off the top board?" He frowned.

"Yes." I added, "That's when I found the gun." Frowning, I crossed my arms.

"Like I said, you sure can pick 'em." He shook his head. "Whose gun, was it?"

"Don't know. I gave it to Don, and his standard reply was 'can't discuss an ongoing investigation.'"

"Yep. Sounds about right." He nodded, his chin and gray ponytail bobbed. "I'll get to work, take the rest of this bad boy off. Have to go to a lumber company for a thick slab." I had been freaked by finding the gun and could have removed the mantel myself. But I held off, rationalizing that with Wayne's careful demo, there wouldn't be any damage to the surround.

"After I finish sweeping the basement, we can head over to Woodworks." Woodworks was the local lumberyard and revered in the area for custom millwork.

I made quick work of the basement clean up, noting the painted floor had flaked with some of the cement worn down into a shallow depression. At the very least, I would need to repaint, and I mentally added that to the list of supplies.

I trekked upstairs where Wayne was cleaning up the debris from removing the mantel. Finished, he grabbed the waste bag, and we headed out. I locked up while he discarded the bag in the roll-off dumpster.

"We can take Matilda," he said.

"Sounds good." I hopped up into his white work van. He had driven the vehicle for as long as I had known him. One time I had asked why he'd named the van Matilda and he shrugged, and said with a grin, "She looks like a Matilda."

We found a parking space in the crowded lot and headed inside. Wayne's eyes lit up, and he inhaled the scent of the different woods as we traversed the aisles of unfinished doors, windows, and sections of moldings.

"This here is what we want," he stood, transfixed, in front of a section. "Six feet of this slab. Either stained or left natural."

"I thought we would stain it to match the rest of the wood and brought a sample," I showed him the small chunk of trim that I'd stuffed into my pocket. "I'll head over to the stains, see if I can find a match." The other option was having a paint store do a custom match, which would take more time. More time meant more money.

"I'll get this cut while you do that," he said, gazing around at the wood. In his element, I could tell he was considering his next home project. It happens with DIY.

I lucked out with matching the stain to the piece of lumber and met up with Wayne, where he loaded the cut wood onto a flatbed cart.

"This should work," I said and showed him the can of stain.

"Looks good," he said. We headed to the checkout, and I paid the bill.

Chapter 20

After our shopping expedition at the lumberyard, we returned to the rehab. We hauled the supplies and the slab for the mantel into the garage where Wayne could sand it, and I agreed to stain it. It was nearing the end of the day, and Wayne asked, "Mind if I take off, Kiddo?"

"Sounds good. You did a great job finding that wood. I'll make a couple of calls and be right behind you."

"You're at the lawman's place this week?"

"Yes. I need a few things, and I'll get cleaned up at home and then head over."

"How's it going with the sheriff?" He grinned.

"Fine." My stomach seized.

"Uh huh," he looked over his round John Lennon style eyeglasses with a twinkle. "It sure is different, I'll bet."

"It is." I grimaced. "I've become so self-sufficient, it's tough to change."

"How's Eddy doing with that? Ya know that guy still loves ya."

"He lost his job again. Lola kicked him out," I said, shaking my head.

"He needs someone to keep him in line," and he guffawed.

"It's going to be Lola." I retorted, adding, "Been there, done that," and I laughed.

"Uh, huh." He winked and grinned. "I'd best be getting back to my honey."

"How is she?"

"Antsy, wants to put this whole deal about Walter behind her. Can't do that 'til they get the lab results."

"Has she been sleep-walking?"

"No. Now it's just plain old insomnia." He laughed, resigned. "Gets up in the middle of the night and stares at the television. She tells me about the stuff they sell overnight."

"Yeah, cook ovens and beauty products." I chuckled. "Sorry about her sleep."

"Yeah. Me, too." He sighed. "But I'll be here tomorrow."

"Yes. Say 'hi' to Gretta." I smiled in relief. I had gotten her name right.

"Will do." He nodded, grinned, and left.

I headed inside and called the sanitation company to arrange for a pickup on the container. Shoving my hand into my pocket, I fingered the frames I had found earlier in the day. On impulse, I dialed Maxim's. I was curious about the woman I had seen entering the building that morning, and even more inquisitive about whether Sean worked in another department.

The main number for Maxim's looked like a toll-free number but was the only number I could find in the Google search on my phone. After listening to the phone tree options, I went for customer service.

"I'm looking for Sean Young. He's in computer tech support. I don't have his direct number."

"There is no one with that name listed in the directory. Is there anyone else that can assist you?"

"No, thank you. I must have the wrong number."

"No problem," the smooth voice answered.

I hung up and dialed again, punching the option for customer help. Getting a different agent would arouse less suspicion. Sure enough, this time a high-pitched voice answered.

"I am calling for Penelope Young. I'm sorry I don't know which department she works in."

"There's no one by that name in our directory." Maxim's must have a script they train operators with.

"Sorry, wrong number," I said, and hung up, sure now that the woman I had seen earlier must have been a fantasy. It was someone that resembled Penelope.

The paper had mentioned another man, Nathan Winner, as a person of interest. I took a gamble and dialed Maxim's again.

"Nathan Winner please." I said to an operator who sounded like a young man.

"One moment, please."

"Nate Winner here, leave your name and number, and I'll get back to you," the sexy tenor voice came.

I hung up, frowning. Winner had been questioned according to the newspaper, and he still worked at Maxim's. That was curious. Why had he been a person of interest? Was he still being looked at? Dottie had said the department cleaned house after the murder, so he must work in another area. I winced, clutching my phone. Dare I call again? Then, would it really make any difference? What I wanted was a conversation with Nathan Winner.

After retrieving my ring from the powder room and gathering Boots, who had been remarkably well-behaved, I headed out. While locking up, Dottie, the neighbor, called from her sidewalk, "Hi, Katelyn, wasn't it?"

I looked up, "Yes. You can call me Kate."

I waited while she huffed, cutting across the lawn, halted in a wheeze, and took a minute to catch her breath.

"How is the house coming?" The stout woman asked. Her eyes glowed and her complexion flushed from exertion. "Pretty kitty!" She spied Boots in his carrier and reached down to pet him. He hissed his displeasure at her fingers inside his crate.

"It's progressing." Viewing her expression, I sensed there was a purpose behind her visit.

"So," her voice dropped. "I saw Sean and Penelope on Sunday. They parked in the driveway and stared at the house."

"They did?"

"Yes. I think they wanted to get out, but I was in the front yard, checking on the tulips and daffodils to see how they weathered the winter." It was always dicey how flowers would bloom in the Spring. My thumb was brown, and I left gardening to those with greener thumbs.

"Okay."

"So, I think they saw me, and stayed put."

"Curious. I found a pair of glasses in the utility room. They're broken." I fished them out of my pocket.

"Oh, yes." She squinted. "Those were Penelope's. Very nice. She has wonderful taste."

"I will call Sean. I would like to get them back to her. Not sure if they can be repaired with a broken temple. So, you didn't talk to them?"

"No. I haven't spoken to them since before they moved. They didn't appear to want to talk on Sunday. And I mind my own business." She sniffed.

"Yes. I can see that." I smiled. "Do you know where Penelope teaches?"

"I think she is a substitute teacher, don't know where. Art programs are the first to get cut in a down economy. Mostly, she worked for a temporary agency, they sent her out on all kinds of jobs. Even worked at Maxim's for a spell. Receptionist, I think. It was great. Sean and she could carpool and have more together time. It's so hard for working couples to have quality time, don't you think?" She paused long enough to exclaim,

"That is a beautiful ring! Are you engaged to be married?"

I blinked, "Yes, to the sheriff. Thank you. So, Penelope worked for a temporary agency?"

"Yes." Dottie didn't miss a beat. She gasped. "The sheriff! When is the wedding?"

"Do you know which company?" I was nosy, much as Dottie was with her questions, and added, "We haven't set a date."

"Let me think, Ace? Ace Temp Agency." Her voice lowered to a whisper. "I heard Sean got the ax from Maxim's. Bad press for the company, you know."

"Uh, huh? You said there was another man that he hung out with?"

"Oh, yes. The looker." She smiled and scrunched her face, recalling, "I haven't seen him here since the news broke. They were a steady threesome. Played on the company softball team. Used to meet here every Thursday, and sometimes on Saturdays. They took Sean's van and Nathan drove his red sports car. Sometimes, he wore these tortoise shell glasses." She giggled. "Probably tried to look more professional, less a model. Anyway, the looker would take Sean one time, Arthur, the next, with the top down." She giggled. "Even took Penelope once. Looked like fun, if you know what I mean."

"Sure."

"If I can't reach Sean about the glasses, maybe I can reach Penelope through her work. Thank you, Dottie. I have to go." Boots had been quiet while Dottie and I had been talking but yowled insistently now.

"Of course. Your cat is so handsome, aren't you," and reached to the carrier, whereupon he hissed at the outstretched hand.

"It was good talking to you." My mind was on overload as I nodded to Dottie and stowed Boots' crate into the SUV. Doubting that a broken pair of glasses would be enough for Sean and Penelope to make the trip to their old residence, I pondered if it could be for the gun I found in the mantel, which was now in Don's possession. Nathan Winner and his red sports car were interesting. No room for the three of them in his car. Sean or Arthur must have driven separately. If Penelope went to the games, Sean must have trusted Nathan and Arthur enough to be alone with her.

Chapter 21

After arriving home, I brought Boots inside, and he darted from his carrier and headed to his favorite spot on the sofa. I left him fresh water and chow while I showered and dressed for Don's house. It was surreal, going from my home to his, and I felt a little like Cinderella would, going to the ball. Esther would have dinner ready, and we may even eat in the formal dining room by candlelight. I nixed that thought being a Monday night, and spring, the time of year where daylight was becoming longer.

Pulling into Don's circular drive, I parked and honked. I didn't have a garage door opener yet. It was on his list. It was likely Esther who hit the remote so that I could enter, and I parked next to the Corvette. I admired the sporty car while unloading Boots, who howled his displeasure at being disturbed. Esther greeted me from the garage entrance.

"Here, let me take Boots. We are becoming old friends, he and I." Boots grumbled as I handed her the carrier. "Well, maybe we have more work to do." She laughed. "I will get him tuna and bring it up. Mr. Williams is working late tonight. He said for me to get your dinner and he will join you as soon as he can."

"All right." I hadn't thought of him not being here when I arrived. "Does that happen a lot, Mr. Williams, er, Don, working late?" I asked, curious.

"It happens. He is a busy man." She shrugged. "Let's get you settled."

"Hum." Caught off guard, I considered passing on that night and heading back home. I was a little peeved he had not called to let me know, or at least had given me the option.

With Esther carrying Boots' carrier, I trekked alongside with my overnight case. Esther motioned me inside the suite and put Boots in a corner of the room. In front of the window was a cat tower.

"Sweet! Boots, a place for you to see outside!"

"Yep. Thought he would like it. I will get the tuna," Esther said. "You and Mr. Boots make yourselves comfortable," she said, and disappeared down the hallway.

"Ooh, Boots, you are a mister, now. With a view of your own." I chuckled. The room was beautiful and quiet. Too quiet. I dug out my phone and hit Don's office number. The window drew me to the view, and I again inhaled the scenery of the lake while I called.

"Sheriff's office. Morgan Clark speaking." A low, sultry voice came. Immediately, the image of the blonde woman in the office photo appeared. The voice did not fit with the image, ice-blue eyes, short hair, and an air of fierceness, and it unnerved me.

"Hello, Morgan. This is Katelyn. I was calling for the sheriff," I said, feeling a flush rising from my neck.

"He is unavailable. Can I take a message?" Her voice kept the sultry tone but had a note of possessiveness.

"Yes. Please ask him to call."

"Certainly." And she hung up. I was mollified by the fact she readily agreed, had not asked for my number, and so must know who I was.

Esther reappeared with a bowl of tuna and fresh water. Her cheerful stance calmed me, and Boots was excited for his meal.

"For dinner, there is a roasted chicken. The sides are a vegetable, salad, and rice or mashed potatoes."

"Wow. A real dinner. Make whatever Mr. Williams likes. I'm not picky."

"He isn't either." She laughed. "It'll be Esther's surprise. Right Boots?"

"Appreciate it." The matronly woman was growing on me. "Whatever you want."

"Did you want to wait for Mr. Williams? I can hold dinner."

"I left a message for him at his office to call me. Let's give it a few minutes until I hear from him. I could use a snack?"

"You got it, cheese and crackers?"

"Perfect." She hustled out. I was going to love having Esther and felt pampered by the friendly housekeeper.

My cell phone rang, and I hurried to answer, "Hi," I was breathless. "So, you got my message?"

"What message?"

"I left a message with Morgan." I hesitated. "For you to call?"

"No message. I wanted to let you know I would be late with all this danged paperwork. I am sorry, Katelyn. It was all last minute, and I got hung up. Go ahead and eat. I'll grab a burger on the way. Make yourself comfortable."

"Any idea of how long it'll be?"

"It'll be late, after nine o'clock. Sorry, Katelyn. I really wanted to be there earlier."

"Of course, I understand. Duty calls." I felt relieved to hear from him, but what had happened with my message with Morgan?

Maybe she went to the bathroom, didn't write it down, forgot. You really must work on your trust issues.

Esther reappeared with a variety of crackers, cheese, sausage, and grapes. "Don, er, Mr. Williams is going to get a burger on the way home. And this is more than enough dinner for me."

"The chicken will keep until tomorrow's dinner," she replied cheerily. "It happens all the time."

"Have you eaten, Esther?"

"No."

"How would you like to join me with a glass of wine and this wonderful spread?"

"Love to." She grinned.

"Let's eat in the kitchen," I suggested. "Less fuss."

We left Boots to investigate his tower and took the food to the kitchen.

"So, does Mr. Williams have many late nights at work?" I asked, nibbling a slice of Havarti cheese. We sat at a table with a view of the lawn, and beyond that, the lake.

"Well, the town is growing. There is more happening, more police work, more paperwork to go with the policing."

"Uh, huh."

"It seems like they add a person, and the work nights get more frequent. Which, if you ask me, should be the opposite. A new person should lighten the load."

"Do you mean Morgan Clark?" I studied Esther. Her direct manner was refreshing.

"She is a real go-getter, that Morgan. Sees crime where nobody did before." She chortled.

"You think she's too aggressive?" My head tilted, speculating.

"It's not for me to say, but some charges she finds are a little out there for a normal officer." Esther pressed her lips together.

"Like what?"

"She ticketed a bicyclist for not stopping at a stop sign."

"That bugs me too," I admitted. "They're supposed to follow the rules of the road." I grimaced.

"Perhaps the bicyclist slowed down, but didn't stop," she suggested.

"What else?" I helped myself to a cracker and topped it with sausage and cheese.

"She's becoming famous for giving tickets for speeding under five miles over, and for under the speed limit," Esther said.

"I always thought five miles over was within the limit."

"Not for Morgan Clark. She will do three miles." She chuckled. "Creates a lot more paperwork."

"But it must add revenue to the town?"

"I would say it's a trade-off. More busy work. I heard about the sleepwalking deal. Throwing someone in the slammer for confessing to a crime while fast asleep. Poor woman was probably having a nightmare."

"You mean Gretta Hamer?"

"Yes. That lady." She layered a cracker with cheese.

"They are waiting on the DNA from Gretta's memory box. I'm sure she will be fine."

"Yep. But what a waste of money and resources!"

"I heard they must investigate because she confessed. If she were awake, she wouldn't confess." I chuckled at the thought of Gretta killing anyone, let alone admitting to the crime.

"Harrumph. Anyway, Ms. Morgan has added a bunch of paperwork to the department." She yawned, and I looked at the time. It was nearing eight o'clock.

"You must be tired, Esther. Boots and I will wait in the family room for Don."

"Sounds good. I'll clean up and go to my room." Esther had a private room with an ensuite in another wing of the mansion. A fact that I had learned on my tour with Don.

"Good night, Esther. Thank you." I headed up to my suite to capture Boots and bring him to the family room. Boots had found the bed and was curled up on a pillow. Snatching him up, I headed back downstairs to the family room to sit in front of the impressive fireplace. There was plenty of sofa room to snuggle, and we waited. The room was spectacular, but I missed my space. My sofa, kitchen, and bedroom.

Eight o'clock, eight-thirty, nine o'clock. Between scrolling on my computer, I checked the time obsessively. At ten o'clock, I took my overnight bag and loaded Boots into his carrier to head home. The car's motor was running when the overhead door to the garage opened, and Don drove in.

I waited while he came to the driver's side, his expression apologetic.

"Sorry, Katelyn, please don't go," he said through the closed window.

I sighed and lowered the window.

"So, this is how it is going to be? Me waiting up for you?" I stared at him.

"No, Katelyn. Not always, it's just been a bad stretch."

"Did Morgan ever tell you I called?"

"Yes, she did. She had gone for more coffee. She told me when she returned."

"All right," I was placated. "But I don't want a life of waiting for someone to come home at night."

"It's not always like that. I am the sheriff. It can get dangerous and there can be long nights."

"Can't you stay in the office and do paperwork from nine to five?"

"I do some work there. But you know how I love going into the community, keeping the peace, meeting the public."

"Yes, I do." I said, leaning back against the seat, feeling deflated. "But I don't want to be here if you're working late again. I would rather stay at my place."

"That's fine, for now," he said.

I raised my brows, "For now?"

"It'll be different once we're married."

"Then I won't have a place to go to."

"Let's not talk about this now, Katelyn. Stay over," he urged. "Besides, I have good news."

"What?"

"The department dropped the investigation into Gretta Hamer. The lab reports on Walter's items came back negative for the poison from Monkshood. She is home free."

"That is wonderful! Do Wayne and Gretta know?" I whooped, and Boots yowled and scratched in his crate at the unexpected sound.

"Yes. It is public knowledge."

"Woo Hoo!" Impulsively, I leaned out of the window and kissed Don, and he kissed me back, leaving me breathless. We retrieved Boots and my belongings and went inside the mansion.

Over a toast to Gretta's freedom, we talked until the wee hours of the morning, warmed by the fireplace in the great room.

Chapter 22

Wayne called while I was packing out from Don's place and asked if he and Gretta could take the day and celebrate her freedom.

"Of course, Wayne! You and Gretta take all the time you want."

"I expect we'll chill and go out to dinner someplace special 'cuz it's not every day you get out of jail. Maybe not jail, but out from under suspicion. You know what I mean." He laughed.

"Not a problem."

"I'll be back to install that mantel tomorrow."

"Sounds good."

After leaving Boots at home in familiar surroundings, it was late morning when I arrived at the renovation. I was on a high from talking to Don the evening before, the late night forgiven. He left the house before I did. Esther had coffee and offered to cook an omelet. I opted for my usual breakfast of strong Colombian coffee and a piece of fruit to go. She poo poohed me. "You need protein. Have a hard-boiled egg."

"Thanks Esther," I sliced and seasoned it. "You are right." I was going to love having the housekeeper around.

I placed my ring in the powder room vanity drawer, as was becoming my habit. With Wayne away, the timing was perfect to stain and varnish the mantel. I brought my work radio into the garage and adjusted the volume. Wayne had placed the wood on two sawhorses, set up for that purpose. I sanded the wood and wiped it clear of dust and, wearing rubber gloves, applied a coat of stain with a cloth. I compared my wood sample with the stain and was satisfied with the match. Leaving it to dry between the coats of varnish, I headed inside.

Taking a breather, I called Myra.

"Hey Myra, how's it going?"

"Fine." She was terse.

"Is something wrong?" It wasn't like Myra to snip.

"I talked to Bernie about Gabriella."

"What did he say?"

"He insists she is the real deal."

"You told him she gave us the same reading? Can't dance with one man and danger with money?"

"Yes." She was short.

"And?" I asked, her silence puzzling.

"He said that she had a 90% accuracy with her clients. They swore by her."

"Really? Our auras might have mingled, if there is such a thing?" I asked.

"Hum, maybe. He could be right," she groused.

"Oh, oh. What happened?"

"Yesterday, the lights started dimming in my bathroom and then in each room."

"No!" Frowning, I said, "Okay, where are you going with this?"

"My entire house needs to be rewired."

"You're kidding!"

"No!" My mind clicked through the expense and inconvenience.

"Yes. I have spent the day contacting electricians and getting bids."

"Myra, you could have my job, a home rehab specialist," I teased.

"It is going to be thousands of dollars. Unexpected money, out the door."

"So, I guess the danger would be in not getting the electrical rewired? The money, of course, is the expense of it all."

"Yes. And that isn't all."

"What else?" I asked, frowning.

"I swear one of the electricians was hitting on me." She harrumphed.

I couldn't help myself and giggled. "Myra, it's never too late for romance."

"It is for me." She was firm. "Anyway, how is it going with Don?"

"All right."

There was silence while Myra digested my scant response.

"He worked late last night, and when I was about to leave, he finally showed. So, I stayed, and we talked." I blathered on, "Good news about Gillie, 'er Gretta. She is testy about the nickname."

"Go on?" she prompted.

"She has been cleared. I don't know all the details, but it sounds like it's over."

"Good. So now they must figure out why she sleepwalks. That is how it started, right?"

"Yes, it is."

I hung up from Myra and chuckled about her home improvement project. DIY had bonded us from the start. We met years earlier at a class on faux finishing when the style was fashionable. We became fast friends, and she had encouraged my move into flipping houses.

I hoped that the reading didn't foretell any more expense than I budgeted. The new carpet had been unexpected, but maybe that cost had already been accounted for in the psychic's reading. One could hope. The 'dance' was different, and the thought of someone other than Don made me squeamish, although a future with Don also made me nervous. Gabriella's accuracy allowed for a 10% error, right?

Chapter 23

In the laundry room, I scrubbed the tub where I had cleaned up after staining the wood, when the house shook from a loud noise. Gasping, I ran to the entry and saw the rear of a blue van pull away from the garage.

"What in the world!" I was in shock while watching the scene unfold.

The driver gunned the engine, reached the end of the driveway, and abruptly stopped. He threw the van into reverse and rammed the garage door again. The fiberglass door shattered. The driver's face contorted as he threw the van into gear and made his getaway, narrowly missing my car. The van's tires squealing, he slowed enough to make the turn to the street and stomped on the accelerator.

Stepping out on the stoop, I fumbled for my cellphone to call 9-1-1, when a squad car pulled into the drive.

"I called the cops." Dottie came huffing across the lawn. "Saw the whole thing. It was Sean!"

Behind her, a female officer hurried from the car and joined us on the sidewalk.

"Officer Morgan Clark here. What happened?" She was sturdy, with broad shoulders. Her stare flicked between us, then focused on me. "Who lives here?"

"I own the house. I am rehabbing it."

"Your name."

"Katelyn Baxter."

"I called the police. My name is Dorothy Barker. People call me Dottie. I live next door." She huffed; her face flushed with excitement.

Behind Morgan's car, the sheriff's car stopped, and Don hopped out and hurried up the sidewalk.

Morgan stepped aside, and Don faced me. "Are you okay? What happened?"

"I can handle this, Sheriff," Morgan said.

"It is okay, Morgan. I will take this." Don nodded to Morgan, and her back stiffened. This could get touchy. I stood, dazed from the scene of the van's driver ramming the garage door. Dismayed, I surveyed the busted door and the side of the garage. My freshly stained mantel lay on the cement floor, dented. The sawhorses were toppled, and one had broken legs.

"It was Sean Young. He was furious and drove into the garage." I shook my head, puzzled.

"You're sure it was him?"

The driver's rage-filled profile was imprinted on my memory.

"I'm positive."

Dottie nodded vigorously. "It was him. He has a temper. I have seen him go off before."

We studied the neighbor, curious.

"He cut down a neighbor's tree because a branch from the tree fell into his yard. Nobody could prove it was Sean because he did it at night. The neighbor knew it had to be him, because he had made such a stink about cleaning up the mess from the fallen branch. It was a nice tree, sugar maple. The leaves have beautiful colors in the fall." She blinked and smiled at the memory of autumn foliage.

"But no one saw him cut down the tree?"

"No. But I saw and heard him cussing while he raked up the mess." Her forehead creased as she recounted the incident.

"Morgan, take a report from Dorothy about Sean Young's activities."

"Yes, Sheriff." Her gaze dimmed. "If you'll follow me." She nodded at Dottie. With a firm stride, she went to the squad car to take the report, with Dottie trailing her.

"I don't understand why he would do this. He doesn't own the house anymore. I haven't done anything. . ." I hesitated and gulped. Don looked at me sharply.

What is it?" he asked.

"Uh, nothing." My paranoia had struck. I had been calling Maxim's, asking for him and for Penelope. Had it gotten back to him?

"Are you snooping again?" His gaze was cool, and I winced.

"No. Well, maybe he thought I was?"

"Katelyn?" His voice was harsh.

"I found a pair of glasses that I thought they may want. I called Maxim's and asked for him." Leaving out the part where I was curious about if he still worked there, or if Penelope was at the same employer. Dottie returned to where we talked while Morgan stayed in the car, finishing her report.

"She said she would call Sean about the glasses," Dottie said, her face flushed from the police attention. "I saw them. They belong to Penelope."

I was glad I had Dottie to back me up, but I wished she would keep quiet.

"Let's see the glasses," Don said.

"They're inside." I entered the house and retrieved them from the kitchen drawer where I had stowed them, then returned to the group. Offering the glasses to Don, I said, "See?"

"I'll take them." My stomach lurched as my excuse for contacting Penelope disappeared.

"Morgan, take photos of the garage for the report." Morgan squared her shoulders, "Yes, sir." Don turned toward me, "I'll see you later." And he stomped off.

"Is that your fiancé?" Dottie squealed. "He's so cute, manly."

"He is." I watched Don Williams get behind the wheel of the sheriff's car and drive away, my stomach sinking. Dottie headed home, and I called the insurance agent.

I reported the vandalism, hoping insurance would cover the damage. I was relieved when the agent said the policy covered damages, less my hefty deductible. The adjuster would be out the next day.

I taped a blue tarp over the damage and space left bare by the collision to the garage door.

It had been a short day, and while heading for home, I grumbled about the damaged house and was not happy about facing Don's questions later that night. My angst increased when I saw Eddy's truck in the parking lot of my townhome. I charged inside.

"Why are you here? How did you get in?" My hair was wild, and my mood matched.

"Take it easy, Katie," Eddy popped up, awakened from a nap. "You scared the devil out of me." He grabbed his chest and sat upright on the sofa. Boots scurried off the back of the couch and ran to the bedroom.

"Answer me!"

"Okay, okay. I had an interview and decided to take a quick nap. I planned to be gone by the time you got home."

My eyes narrowed. "In my house, on my sofa? Have you been sneaking in all along?"

"No, I have not been sneaking in. I used a key."

"How? If I remember correctly, I took that key back." Once upon a time, I had given Eddy a key in case of emergency, and I had taken it back under similar circumstances.

"Oh, yeah. I used your spare from under the doormat." He ruffled his hair. I had duct-taped a spare under my welcome mat for emergencies. Note to self: find a new hiding spot.

"Eddy!"

"Don't yell, Katie. It's not nice." He rubbed his eyes. "It was just today. Lola's still mad at me."

"I want the key." I held out my hand while Eddy plucked it out of his shirt pocket. Then the absurdity of the day hit me, and I started giggling uncontrollably. I regained my composure. Eddy snickered, and that set me off on another wave of laughter.

Squelching my giggles, I sat on the easy chair facing him.

"Eddy, I am engaged to be married. You have a relationship with Lola. Our lives have changed. We are not teenagers anymore."

He sat with his head between his hands and said quietly, "You're right, Katie."

"I know I am. How was your interview?"

"Second interview. They will let me know."

His cellphone sounded, and he left the living room while he answered. I heard murmurings and parting words that sounded like 'thank you,' and then he returned.

"Woo Hoo!" He grabbed my arms and lifted me from the chair in a bear hug. "I got the job. I start Monday!"

"That's great, Eddy."

"Let's celebrate, Katie! Ivan's?"

"I'm at Don's tonight, remember?"

"Oh, yeah." He stood back and gazed at me with his big brown eyes through long eyelashes. "How about one last dinner?"

It was early. I could have dinner with Eddy and still get to Don's before too late. I was wrung out from the disaster of the day at the rehab and not looking forward to his questions about my inquiries about Sean and Penelope. What could one night out hurt?

"All right, Eddy. An early dinner, and that's it. You are going home to Lola."

"Sure thing, Katie." I ignored the sparkle in his eyes.

***

I should have known better. After one glass of wine, I had another. Before I knew it, I had unloaded to Eddy about the current state of the rehab and Don's disapproval about my flipping houses, and of course, my delving into another murder mystery. Did Sean kill his coworker and dump him in a field? Was it an angry lover? Or the mystery man, Nathan Winner?

Before I knew it, I had had a third glass of wine, and Eddy and I were singing and swaying along to Ivan's Tuesday night karaoke singers. Eddy was a tall guy and could handle a couple of drinks. Me, not so much. It was ten o'clock when he left me at my door, and I cringed at the time. I dug out my cell phone and peered at the face. There were two missed calls from Don. I hadn't heard the phone while I had been at Ivan's commiserating with Eddy. I collapsed on the sofa and dialed Don.

"Katelyn! Where are you?" Don asked, sounding worried.

"I went out and lost track of time. I'm sorry," I said, wincing at the concern in his voice.

"Have you been drinking?" he asked. He sounded wary.

"Yes."

"Well, don't drive," he said, firmly.

"I won't." There was silence while I braced myself for the next question, like did you drive home, or who did? Relief and guilt swept over me when he said, "It was a rough day. I got scared when I didn't hear from you. I'm glad you're okay. We will talk tomorrow. Get some rest." He clicked off.

Sobering up from his tone, I looked over at Boots, as guilt washed over me.

"Why am I being a jerk?" He gave his opinion by wrinkling his nose and curling up. Glancing down at my hand, I realized with a start I had forgotten my engagement ring at the rehab.

Chapter 24

Reality set in the next day at the project. The outside was a disaster. After I surveyed the garage, I headed to the basement to review my work there. While mentally tallying the damage, I detoured upstairs to the powder room where I had left the diamond ring in a vanity drawer.

"Huh?" I abruptly halted, startled as Dottie hid her hand, a flash of the diamond catching my eye. Dottie saw that I had seen the gem and quickly held out her hand. "I'm sorry, it's just so beautiful. I had to try it. Please forgive me." The jewel sparkled on her finger. Her face was contrite. She slipped it off and handed it to me. "It's a wonderful ring, Katelyn. I'm thrilled for you."

My stomach plummeted when I assessed the scene and thought the worst. Gathering my wits and seeing that she was sorry, I said, "It's all right, Dottie. It is a beautiful ring. I thought it would be safer if I left it in a drawer, rather than wearing it while I work. I meant to leave it at home." I saw a fleeting look of guilt cross her face.

"You got in through the garage?" I asked.

She nodded and sniffled, dabbing her nose. "I was going to yell, but my nose started dripping. I was looking for a tissue. Allergies." She sniffed again. "I know, I should have used toilet paper instead of going through drawers," she blithered, her face reddened, and she grabbed a square from the roll. "I should go," she said, rubbing her nose. She grabbed another square of paper and hurried away, leaving me stunned, watching after her.

I examined the ring and vigorously polished it, feeling guilty for leaving the gem unattended. Slipping it on my finger, I felt a wave of relief.

I wasn't wild about stowing it there but was more uncomfortable forgetting it at a job. After considering putting it in my messenger bag, I nixed the idea, concerned the bag could be lost or stolen. My pocket felt deep enough to store it short term and I slipped it inside. From here on out, I vowed to leave the gem at home when I went to work.

The insurance adjuster came by and assessed the damages. They had a figure in mind, and it came short of what I believed it would cost to fix it. I called the contractors and asked Wayne to look at the side of the garage. Most of the damage to the house was to one side, and the overhead door was toast.

"He mangled the frame. The whole kit and caboodle will have to be replaced. The side of the garage can be fixed, but it will have to match the siding. Looks like he just missed the corner support."

"Thanks Wayne."

"Get estimates from three contractors. That should cover anything I missed."

"Called them already. They are on their way."

"What's the guy's beef?" Wayne asked. He frowned.

"Not sure, he just showed up and battered the garage. He has a temper." I didn't want to get into what could have set off Sean with Wayne.

"Uh, huh. Lucky you weren't inside the garage when it happened."

"Yes. It was."

"So, you want me to get another piece of wood for the mantel?" His eyes lit up, and I figured he was recalling the fun he had going through the wood selection at the lumberyard.

"Yes. That would be good." I could keep working inside while the outside was sorted out with the damages. I headed to the basement to paint the flaked cement in the utility room. As I sanded the floor to remove any paint before recoating, I considered my plan to contact Penelope with the pretext of the found glasses. Now that Don had them, I couldn't call with the weak excuse of finding them, considering they were broken and likely forgotten, but it niggled at me. Did Sean break the glasses in a fit of anger? If so, why? I considered calling Ace, the temporary agency.

Myra's steady voice sounded official enough to convince someone that they needed a reference on an employee. The scene with Dottie in the bathroom nagged at me. Also needed was a sober talking to about my antics of the last evening. Myra could do that, too. I pulled out my phone and sat on a rung on the stairs and dialed.

I discussed the scene with Myra.

"You think she would have kept the ring?" she asked.

"Lord, I hope not." I gulped. "She handed it over right away."

"Tissue boxes are usually left out. She went through drawers?"

"It was dusty from the work in the house. She may have thought there would be tissues in a drawer?"

"I'd give her the benefit of the doubt. It is a beautiful gem, and if she was looking for a tissue, and spotted the ring, it was an impulse to try it on. If the ring went missing, you would know it was her. Plus, she knew you were in the house."

"That's true," I admitted.

"But you need to be more careful," she chided.

"Yes, Myra. I'll take more care. Thanks for listening."

"It's what friends do."

"Hey, Myra, I do have a favor to ask." I explained my mission, and she asked the obvious.

"Why do you want to talk to Penelope? Was she in the van that rammed the garage?"

"No. He was alone."

"So?" she asked.

"I'm not sure. If Sean has a temper, and the broken glasses are a result of their relationship, she could know something about the murder?"

"And, because the house belonged to him, you think it's tainted because any prospective buyer has to be informed if a violent death occurred in the residence?"

"It's the law in Minnesota."

"Yes. It is. I will see what I can do."

"I would like to know if she is on a job for the temp agency. If she is working some place as a receptionist, I could walk in."

"And do what? Introduce yourself? Ask if her husband murdered Arthur Cook? Or did she? You have guts." She groaned.

"I'll think of something," I said.

"I believe you will." She chuckled. "How's the wedding planning going?"

"Myra, I am so scared. Not to mention in the doghouse. I went out with Eddy last night."

"You what!" She inhaled.

"It wasn't like that. It's complicated. He got a job, and we went to Ivan's to celebrate. I had too much wine, and we swayed to the music."

"Sway, like in dance?"

"Close, sort of, I don't know. . ." I wailed.

"Sounds like Gabriella's reading is right on. I'm still trying to ditch the electrician," she muttered.

"Now, that's interesting," I teased.

"No. It is not. It's a curse we need to undo. I will see what Bernie says. It sounds as though Don is being considerate. He isn't pushing you?"

"He is a nice guy," I said, echoing her sentiments about Sheriff Don Williams.

"He totally is."

"Let me know what you find out. I had better get back to work."

Hanging up, I returned to prepping the floor when there was a loud knock at the front door. I headed upstairs and answered. Don stood on the stoop, the silver strands in his blond hair catching the sunlight.

"Katelyn, I thought we could go to lunch." His gaze was sober. "It's one o'clock."

"Let me wash up and get my bag." I took a quick detour to the bathroom and freshened up. "How about the sub sandwich place?" I called, as I gathered my things. "It's close." Anyplace but Ivan's. After scribbling a note for Wayne, I got in the front seat of the sheriff's car.

We made small talk on the way to the deli.

"Nice day," I said. The midday sunbathed the trees and spring smelled of fresh lilacs.

"Uh, huh."

"Has Sean been charged with the vandalism?" I asked.

"Morgan is working on it. She will track his vehicle and see if there is any damage that would tie him to the incident. Property crimes are not high priority, and no one was hurt."

"Morgan appears to be very capable."

"She is." He nodded.

We rode in silence the rest of the way to the eatery. After placing our orders, we picked them up and sat at a counter overlooking the parking lot. After a few comments about the weather, I grew uneasy, and squirmed in my seat. Then, with a solemn expression, he asked, "What happened last night?"

"I am sorry I didn't call. It was a spur-of-the-moment thing. I didn't see that you called until I got home. It won't happen again." I flushed red.

"You went out alone?"

"Eddy wanted to go out and celebrate his new job. I didn't think it would get late." I squirmed again.

"You went out drinking with Eddy, your ex-husband?"

I swallowed a bite of sandwich that felt dry in my mouth.

"Yes. Eddy is my ex-husband. He is a friend now. Nothing more." I said evenly, matching his gaze.

"Uh, huh." I watched his eyes travel to my hand, and I tensed. "I put the ring in my pocket while I worked this morning." Reaching into my jean pocket, I felt for the gem. He placed his hand on my arm.

"No. Keep it there." He glanced sideways at me.

"What does that mean?" I stiffened.

"I want you to keep the ring safe until we sort out what's going on."

"I don't follow. If this is about Eddy and my being out late, well, forget it. You kept me waiting until late-night the day before. You didn't even call!"

"I was working. It isn't the same thing."

"Well, late is late!" I stood up, ready to leave.

He paused, and his eyes went soft. "I should have called earlier. I am sorry."

I sat down again. His words soothed me.

"I said it was a rough day, didn't I?" He threw up his hands. My glance went to the couple watching behind the sandwich prep station. They turned away. Three more customers entered the shop.

"Was last night payback for my working late?" he asked quietly.

"No!" I stopped and thought. I shook my head. "It wasn't."

"Okay." He didn't sound convinced.

"Eddy is safe," I admitted, and nibbled at the sub sandwich.

"And I'm not?" his eyebrows lifted. He put his sandwich down and wiped his hands with a napkin.

"Not exactly." I gulped. "You are change. I hate change."

"Now you're scaring me." He placed his hand over mine. I felt eyes from the food station behind us again. Shifting, I blocked their view. "What do you want to do?" The warmth of his touch sent tingles up my neck.

"I'm not sure." Grimacing, I pushed my food away. "It isn't working for me to stay at your place. At least, not during the week."

"I get that." He nodded, soberly.

"Boots does not like change either. But he appreciates the cat tower." I tried to lighten the mood.

"Huh." He smiled briefly and gazed sideways at me and sipped of his cola. "Let's trade weekends for now?"

"Your turn to stay at my place this weekend," I said.

"You got it. Now, put on the ring."

I reached into my pocket and slipped it on. He leaned over and kissed me. There was a small cheer from the counter staff and two more customers. We locked gazes, laughed, and nodded. Finished with our food, we left. The sun was bright, and I breathed in the fresh air.

"I'll walk back to the renovation from here," I said. "Stretch my legs. It is a gorgeous day."

His cell phone rang, and he said, "I'm wanted back at the office. We will talk later." We exchanged a brief kiss, aware that the people inside the deli were watching.

    I needed to process what had happened, clear my head, and took off at a brisk pace. We had compromised on how to merge our lives. Baby steps, I reasoned, approaching the renovation.

Chapter 25

Wayne was back from the lumberyard and sat on the steps, smoking a Camel unfiltered cigarette.

"Hope you weren't waiting too long. Don took me to lunch."

"Nope, got the new piece for the mantel." He nodded toward the back of his open truck. "Figured you'd be back soon. Your car's here." He grinned. "How was lunch?" He stubbed out his smoke and stood, stuffing his hands into his jacket.

"Good." I nodded.

"Was that Eddy's truck I saw in the parking lot yesterday?" He squinted.

"Let's not go there."

"Sure enough. Change is tough."

"Yes. It is." I pressed my lips together and nodded. "I'll keep working on the basement floor."

"Can we go ahead with the repairs?"

"I don't see why not. The insurance company has assessed the damages. I will pay you what they pay? Unless it isn't enough?"

"That'll work." He nodded. "I'll shore up the corner of the garage. The garage door company will have to replace the door."

"Yes. Sounds like a plan."

I headed to the basement, slipping my ring into my pocket. Tomorrow for sure I will leave the rock at home. It's safer.

After scraping the flaked cement paint from the floor and studying the area, I decided I would have to recoat the entire floor and cleaned the area. Sean had said there was water damage from a failed sump pump in last year's spring rains. He had not repainted the floor. The area was soft and crumbly under the flaked paint, and I considered whether to patch with quick cement. I decided against it; the shallow impression would look better after a paint job. And the furnace and water softener along with storage made it a utility room, not part of the finished basement.

I got as close to the water softener and furnace as possible. On my hands and knees with a scrubber, a reddish-brown dried color behind the softener caught my attention. A chill traveled my spine. Curious, I dabbed my sponge at the spot, then halted, seeing more specks further up on the back of the softener. Slowly, I backed out.

I ran up the steps and into the garage where Wayne had repaired the wooden sawhorse and was in the process of nailing in a new corner stud.

"Wayne, can you come downstairs? I want you to see this."

"Sure thing." He put down his hammer and followed me to the utility room.

"What do you think this is?" I pointed to the spots.

He squatted and went down on one knee, peering behind the water softener. Wetting his finger, he wiped one dot of brownish red. He smelled his finger and then wiped it on the sponge I had left in my haste.

"Looks like it could be blood."

"Dang it!" I viewed the area. The utility room walls hadn't been finished with drywall, and the studs that framed the room and the ceiling rafters were visible.

"Maybe it was an accident someone caught their arm or leg on a nail in the studs next to the water softener. There are a few that stick out."

"That could be it." Wayne said. Our gazes met.

"You think I should call the police?" My shoulders slumped.

"Yep." He stood and scanned the floor behind the softener.

"Okay." Grimly, I reached for my phone. He left the room as I dialed. "Thanks, Wayne," I said, and I took a deep breath.

I dialed Don direct.

"Sheriff Williams' phone, Morgan Clark here." This was getting annoying. I bit my lip before I asked, "Is the sheriff available?"

"He is in a meeting. How can I help you?" Her manner was brisk.

"Ask him to call Katelyn, please." I questioned my decision to wait for Don's call, with the thought that if it was blood, it had been there a while. If it had been missed, it could wait.

"Certainly." She clicked off, an edge to her tone.

I went upstairs and outside to where Wayne sat on the stoop and had lit a smoke. He blew a ring of smoke into the air.

"I left a message for Don to call," I said and sat down next to him.

"The investigators did a thorough search of the house. Doesn't seem like they would have missed it," Wayne said.

"Maybe they didn't. Sean was in a hurry to sell. He was rushed in clearing out and clean-up," I added.

"Uh, huh." He nodded.

The minutes passed in what seemed an eternity. I thought of the damages to the house that were unexpected. The new carpeting that followed the carpeting Sean had installed. The gun I had found hidden away in the mantel and the broken glasses that Don took. Damage to the garage and now more blood? Was this house a site of a murder? This was not going well. Was Don right? Should I give up rehabbing properties? My track record wasn't encouraging.

"How's Gretta doing?" I steered my thoughts away from my problems.

"She's good. Seeing a therapist for her sleepwalking."

"Good."

"Yep. Scared her, getting busted for Walter's death."

"I'll bet. I am glad that is done."

"Me, too!" He snorted and stubbed out his Camel, stripping the paper. He rose, and I got up from the hard cement steps.

"You don't have to hang out, Wayne. It is almost four o'clock, and I'll wait a few more minutes for his call. If he doesn't respond, I will head out, too," I said.

"You sure?"

"Positive."

"I'll get going, then." He left after closing the house and taping the tarp on the side of the garage. He had repaired the corner, and the door would arrive the next day.

I kept checking my phone for Don's call. Giving up, I motored out.

It was after seven o'clock that night when Don called.

"How was your day?" he asked.

"You didn't get my message?"

"What message?"

"The one I left with Morgan for you to call."

"She must have forgotten. Did you say it was important?"

"Any call I make asking for a return call is important." I was getting hot.

"I'll talk to her."

"Do that!"

"What happened?"

"I found spots that look like blood in the rehab's basement."

"My investigators thoroughly examined and took all evidence." He was testy, and I snapped back. "They could have missed it. It was behind the water softener in the basement."

"Katelyn, they took samples of all the blood evidence," he said firmly. "In the bedroom, hall, and basement."

"The basement? Whose blood is it!"

"I can't discuss an ongoing case."

"I'm going to hang up now," I said. And I clicked off. "Would have been nice if he'd said earlier that there was blood in the basement," I muttered. Boots looked at me from his perch on the couch, licked his paws, and closed his eyes.

Frustrated, I called Myra to vent.

"So, they know about the blood in the basement, too," Myra said.

"Apparently."

"What else?"

"What do you mean?"

"Something's bugging you, I can tell," she said. "More pre-wedding nerves?"

"It seems impossible to merge our lives, Myra. He has all this wealth, and he doesn't want me to rehab houses," I blurted. "Now, his deputy isn't giving him my messages."

"What?"

"Morgan 'forgets' to give him my calls," I muttered. "We had a nice lunch today and decided changing off during the week wasn't working, so it's just weekends now. But when I found more blood, I wanted to tell him. Left a message. He didn't get it."

"What do you know about Morgan?"

"She is ambitious. But forgetful," I added sarcastically.

"He needs to fix that," she said. "She's likely doing that with all his calls. I will have my brother try him, see what happens."

"If he discovers he isn't getting his messages from the police chief, that will get his attention." I snickered.

"Yes, it will. I'll let you know. So, he said the blood was examined?"

"Yes. I have not seen blood anywhere else in the basement, so I believe we are talking about the same blood. I'm curious about Penelope. Don took the broken eyeglasses I found."

"I called Ace Temporary Agency today." Myra's voice held a lilt.

"You did? Awesome! What did they say?"

"I called asking about Penelope Young for my small start-up company and hinted I might want someone on a temporary basis. Okay, I stretched the truth."

"No company, start-up, or not," I said.

"You got it. I said someone had recommended her, and what could they tell me?" She went on. "Penelope had glowing recommendations. But they said she was on a long-term, temporary assignment. And they offered another name, of course."

"Did they say where she worked?"

"No. But I would say the chances are good that Maxim's is your company."

"Makes sense. Dottie said she worked as a temp there, and I saw her. But I wasn't sure." I recalled the morning on the way home from Don's. "I wonder what department? The company operator couldn't find her listed."

"You called Maxim's?" she asked.

"Yes."

"Temp employees may be different. They come and go?" Myra suggested. "You could follow her in some morning?"

"That would be tricky. There is a lot of security, cameras, guards checking ID's, and electronic keypads," I said.

"You could hang out in the parking lot, wait for her to get off work, and talk to her then?" she suggested.

"Myra, you are a cagey one. I am impressed."

"I do what I can. Now, if I could just get rid of the electrician." She harrumphed.

"He's still around?"

"He keeps insisting he needs to check the wiring."

"Maybe he does?"

"He brings donuts and coffee." Her voice was sweet.

"That's nice."

"He wants to chat," she said, flatly.

"He's friendly and lonely?" I offered.

"I'm not. Just check the wiring and be gone, I say," she said, exasperated.

"Harsh." I commented. "You'll figure it out. He might be a good guy?" I hung up with a giggle. Myra with a beau who is an electrician? It could work.

Chapter 26

The sound of Nathan Winner's sexy tenor on Maxim's voicemail tweaked my curiosity. He had been part of the group with Arthur, Sean, and Penelope. Was he involved with the co-worker's murder? Dottie said the men played on the company's softball team. The games were on Thursdays and Saturdays, and they went to Ivan's for a beer and comradery afterwards.

Sports were never my strong suit, but I could catch a fly ball, and I knew how the game was played. I considered going to a game at Maxim's Park, which was named after the employer. I dissed that idea in favor of checking out the players at Ivan's after the game. The company's operator didn't find Sean or Penelope Young in their directory, but the other person of interest, Nathan Winner, still worked for Maxim's. It was a company-wide team, but it could be iffy that he still played. Especially if they were the chummy group that Dottie observed.

It was a Thursday game night, and I considered asking Myra or Don to go. I settled on Eddy because he was comfortable in a bar with a group of ball players. Myra demurred, and I didn't want to tell Don what I was up to.

Dottie, my informant, had given me a sketchy description of Nathan, saying that he was a looker and wore glasses to make him look less a model, and more serious. With any luck, they wore jerseys with their names embroidered on the back. I wondered how he took

Arthur's promotion. Was he up for the same job? If so, how did he take Arthur's ascent to management?

***

Eddy was enthusiastic about having a beer at Ivan's, especially since I was paying.

"I'll have a Nordeast," he told the young server.

"Chardonnay." I ordered. The cheerful woman, sporting green hair and a rose tattoo, slipped away. I noted Katarina was not working the happy hour shift. This gal was a welcome change from the dour server.

"This is so cool, Katie. I get to do some snooping with you," Eddy gushed. "What do we want to find out?"

"I want to talk to him, get a handle on whether he had anything to do with Arthur Cook's murder. But keep your voice down, Eddy. I don't want anyone else to know I'm looking for Nathan Winner," I warned him.

My voice was low, and he shook his head, "Can't hear you."

The din of noise increased as players from Maxim's softball team trouped in. The players jostled one another in loud voices. One said, "great game," as another slapped another player on the back. They took over a long table next to ours, and I studied the men. Most were of average height, within an inch or so. Most had various shades of brown hair poking out from under softball hats with logos of Maxim's. All were tan from hours in the sun, with sturdy builds.

Our table was adjacent, and I had a clear view of some of their backs. Breathing a sigh of relief, I noted that they did wear jerseys with their names. I scanned them and frowned. No Winner.

"What did you say?" Eddy asked. His voice rose above the din.

"Nothing," I said, inwardly pleading he would lower his voice.

I continued to study the players. Then a tall man with sunglasses caught my eye. He swooped in and sat at the end of the table. I observed him, not sure. Most of the men wore similarly shaped glasses with lenses that changed from light to dark in the sun. The lenses had transitioned to clear inside as they sat. Then he removed his hat, and I inhaled. He had a full head of strawberry blond hair. I poked Eddy who sat across from me. He leaned toward me.

"I think that's him on the end." I whispered into his ear. "Look over there." I tilted my head. "Try to look casual."

He glanced over, took a swig of his beer, "Yep. That's your guy."

"I'm going to check out the back of his shirt," I whispered. I rose and read the lettering as I rounded the table to the restroom. "Winner" the jersey read. Nodding, I looked back at Eddy and proceeded to the restroom. Satisfied, I waited inside the bathroom, futzing with my hair. Even as a person of interest in Arthur's murder, he remained at Maxim's and played on the softball team.

Had he remained friends with Sean after Arthur's death? I considered how to approach him or broach the murder. I headed back to the table and stopped short. Eddy had pulled up a chair next to Nathan Winner and sat back chatting with the group.

"Here she is." He spotted me and held up his beer. "This is the woman who is rehabbing Sean Young's house. Katie, have a seat." He pulled up an empty chair next to Nate. "I told him you're redoing Sean's house and we've been talking about the murder. These guys all work for Maxim's. Nate here, worked in the same IT department as Sean." He grinned; his eyes sparkled. Inwardly, I groaned, trying to keep my cool. Grabbing my wineglass, I sat in the chair wedged between Nate and Eddy.

"Nice to meet you." I looked over at Eddy, my brows lifted. I cleared my throat and addressed Nate, "So, you worked with Sean Young and Arthur Cook?"

Nathan had a slow smile, like Robert Redford in an old movie. His top lip lifted, his jaw was firm, and long lashes fringed friendly blue eyes. He was a flirt, and I felt a brief flutter as he held my gaze. This guy is hot. I calmed my nerves and flushed. "What do you think about Arthur and what happened to him?"

"It's too bad what happened to Arthur. He was good at his job," Nate said. "He was better than Sean or me at managing the group. He wasn't very popular. Managers should be competent and likeable." He dipped his chin with an air of confidence.

"You were in the running for management, too?" I asked, noting his tone was a touch arrogant.

"Yes, I was. Sean really wanted the promotion." Nate chewed his bottom lip, a twinkle in his gaze, his voice smooth and casual. "I'm not that ambitious." He took a drink of his beer, and I admired his fluid moves.

"Arthur, Sean, and I were buddies for a while. When Arthur was killed, I kept my distance. It was a shock. I can't believe Sean had anything to do with it."

"But you think he might have?" I ventured.

"Yeah, I do." He laughed in a low, sexy tone. "I know I didn't."

"You don't mess around, do you?" I blinked, stunned.

"Nope." Another chin dip. He met my gaze squarely, and the flirt was gone, and steel replaced the cool blue in his stare. The change was unsettling.

"I have to go," one of the seated players stood. "Me, too," another said. One by one they all rose and pushed back their chairs, and within minutes, all the men were gone.

Nate finished his beer, stood, and said, "Good luck with your house renovation." The mask was up again, the flirt was back. One final dip of his chin, a lazy smile, and he left. Eddy and I were alone, sitting at the long table, and the server started clearing the empty bottles.

"Eddy, why did you tell him what I do?" I whispered. "It's supposed to be a covert operation. I didn't want him to know who I am."

"You found out what you wanted, right?"

"Maybe." The steel in those baby blues lingered.

"I doubt he did it, Katie. He said Arthur was the better man for the job, and he wasn't ambitious. What more is there?"

"He didn't seem to want the job," I admitted. "If you believe him."

"I believe him." Eddy rose, and I did as well. Taking the last sip of wine, I set the glass on the table, whereupon the server scooped up the empty glass and Eddy's bottle.

I believed Nate Winner didn't want the promotion, too. He was way too handsome and hot to care if he was a manager. How did Penelope get along with Nate? If he was buddies with her husband and he flirted with her the way he had with me, how did that float with Sean or Penelope?

Chapter 27

The garage door installer arrived early in the day and replaced the door. The new opener had a different security code to prevent anyone from entering. An ounce of precaution is worth a pound of prevention. So said my paranoia, recalling Sean's unannounced entry with the remote early on. He had bashed the door in anyway, but a new owner would appreciate the system.

Wayne and I left the rehab at the same time. Still curious whether Penelope's temp job was at Maxim's, I drove there, arriving at 4:15 that afternoon. The parking lot had thinned out by 4:45, and I monitored the steady stream of employees and visitors as they left. Slouched in my SUV with the visor down and sunglasses concealing my eyes, I had parked in an inconspicuous spot with a clear view of the doors. My attention peaked when a battered blue van pulled up to the sidewalk, stopped, and a long-legged Penelope got in.

"Sean?" I gasped. I hadn't expected he would pick her up at her job. Dismayed, I watched the van drive off. That ended my plan of catching her on the fly leaving work. I dialed Don.

"Sheriff's office, Morgan Clark here." Figures. I bit my lip.

"Morgan. This is Katelyn Baxter. I just saw the van that rammed my renovation house leave the parking lot of Maxim's."

"Katelyn, we have determined that Sean owns the van in question. We will continue to investigate."

"Uh, huh."

"Did you want to speak to the sheriff?"

"Yes, please." I bit my lip, irritated. It felt like she was micromanaging his calls.

"Katelyn, what are you doing at Maxim's?" Don's voice was terse.

My heart sunk, and I muttered, "Sorry, bad connection. I'll call later." Flushed, I grumbled, "Well, that went well. Not."

Humbled, I drove home, muttering, "What's to investigate? Sean has not fixed the van. There was blue paint on my rehab house, garage door, and the support corner. Dottie and I both saw him. Grrr." I parked, leaving my Ford in the lot to the townhomes, expecting to run errands after dinner. All heck broke loose while I was getting settled.

Rat-a-tat, rat-a-tat. Wayne's knock was loud, followed by yelling, "Kiddo, you got to come outside!"

I ran to the door and threw it open. Wayne's face was anxious, and he gasped. "There's some guy beating the dickens out of your car!"

We ran out together and saw the back of a blue van with a broken taillight racing away, tires squealing, bouncing over a speed bump in a hasty getaway.

"It's Sean Young!"

"Who?" Wayne asked.

"The man I bought the house from," I said.

"That guy they think killed his coworker?"

"The same. What did you see?"

"Me and Gretta was coming back from the store, and he was beating on your car with a tire iron, big as life. Couldn't believe it! I rushed her in, and then banged on your door!"

"Did you call 9-1-1?"

"Nope."

"I'll call."

***

Morgan Clark arrived first. She approached Wayne and me as we stood by my sorry-looking SUV.

"What happened?" she asked, pulling out a pad and pen.

"Sean Young was thrashing Kiddo's car here," Wayne said. "With a tire iron."

"Kiddo?" Her brows lifted as she focused on Wayne.

"Katelyn," he corrected.

"This is your car?" Morgan turned her gaze on me, a challenge in her attitude.

"Yes, it is. I was inside when it happened. Wayne saw the whole thing."

"It was that guy who was supposed to have killed his coworker! I saw him! Stubby guy with a crew cut. Mad as heck, he was. Katelyn recognized his van."

Don drove up then and joined the three of us.

"Didn't you have a run in with Sean Young at another location, just recently?" Morgan asked.

"Yes. She did," Don chimed in, and sent me a resigned look. He nodded. "Hey, Wayne."

"Sheriff," he nodded.

"Yes. He rammed the house I bought from him with his van." I grimaced. "Hit the garage."

"Uh, huh." She asked, "Did anyone else see this happen?"

"Gretta, my wife did," Wayne said. "I'll get her." He left and came back with the petite woman, who wore a yellow hoodie and sweatpants.

"It was unbelievable! We drove in and this man was cussing and swinging this iron bar, breaking windows and what not! Such a scene. I felt sorry for that woman who was with him. She looked terrified," Gretta exclaimed.

"There was someone else in the van?" Don asked.

"Yes. Pretty woman. Her eyes were huge, and she looked scared. She looked like a sophisticated lady." Gretta lifted her chin, reflecting.

"Penelope," I said.

"Katelyn, how would you know who was with him?" Don asked. "You were inside?"

"Just a guess," I gulped. Blushing furiously, I added, "It fits her description. Seems logical."

"I got this," Don said. "I'll finish up here, Morgan. Sounds like dispatch is calling." A crackling sound from the squad car interrupted our gathering.

"Yes, Sheriff." Morgan headed to the police car.

"Looks like another insurance matter, Katelyn," Don said. "We'll take photographs and make a report." While he wrote down all the information from Wayne and Gretta, I listened intently to their accounts. Avoiding Don's gaze, I considered what to say to my agent about another report. Somewhere in my memory bank about insurance was a warning about too many claims within a certain time, they could drop you.

After Don sorted out the incident with Gretta and Wayne, they went inside. With his lips pursed, he squinted at me. Then he took pictures of my mangled car.

"Is there anything you want to add, Katelyn?" His voice was heavy. "Like what you were doing at Maxim's shortly before the trouble here?"

"Not really." Shrugging, I did my best to look wide-eyed and innocent. While Don was questioning Gretta and Wayne, I brought out a waste bag and started cleaning up the shattered glass. After clearing the area around the car, I waited.

"You can't stay here tonight," he said, finished with the couple.

"Yes. I can." Lifting my chin, I met his stare.

"I don't want you to." He said firmly. "Do not make this hard, Katelyn. This guy is mad at you. I want you and Boots to stay with me tonight."

"We just changed it to weekends."

"This is an exception. Ticking off people and an assault on your car at your home is dangerous."

"All right." He had a point.

"I have to call the insurance people again. What about Wayne and Gretta?"

"I think they will be okay. The assault was directed at you. You can call the insurance company from my house."

"I'll pack my bag." I shrugged, secured the garbage bag, and started for my place.

"I'll keep you company while you pack," he said.

"Knock yourself out."

"Katelyn." He was solemn.

"I'm sorry. I know you are trying to protect me." Clutching the refuse in one hand, I pivoted and placed my free arm around his back. He leaned in, folded my body against his chest, and tucked my head under his chin.

"I am worried," he said. We stood huddled together for a minute. Releasing him, I detoured to the dumpster by the garage stalls across from the townhome entry and disposed of the bag of glass shards.

When I returned from my chore, he draped his arm around my shoulder, and we strolled inside. I packed my overnight case and herded a sulky Boots into his carrier. We were quiet, preoccupied with our thoughts, while he drove to his house. I dreaded making another insurance claim and considered how much it would cost to fix the car. My guess was that it would be more than my deductible.

Esther met us at the entry to the estate with a wide smile and a treat for Boots. She slipped the nibble into the carrier.

"Welcome! Sorry to hear about the... incident?" She raised her brows, tactfully avoiding the description of my car being battered.

"Thanks Esther," I smiled gratefully. With the graciousness of the housekeeper and serenity of the surroundings, I felt myself unwind.

"What time would you like dinner?" she asked. "It's meatloaf and mashed potatoes."

"I'm famished," I said. "I love meatloaf!"

"As soon as possible. I'll get Katelyn settled and we will meet you in the dining room. Thank you, Esther," Don said.

"You're welcome."

He grinned. "Esther makes a great meatloaf. We should hurry."

"Sounds good. I will get changed and feed Boots."

"By the way," he grinned. "Myra's brother called today and congratulated me on our engagement."

"He did, did he? And you answered the call? It wasn't Morgan?" I batted my lashes.

"She picked up the phone and handed it to me," he said. "Be sure to thank Myra. It's not often the police chief calls."

"I will." So, Morgan gives him his calls when he's right there. Sort of an answer.

He left, giving me a hug and patting my shoulder.

I took a twirl around the room, feeling a little like Cinderella. Then I changed and fed Boots in record time. Calling the insurance company could wait until tomorrow.

Chapter 28

The next morning, Don left me and Boots at my townhome with a promise to check in later. I would get a ride with Wayne to the rehab. After viewing the damage to my car and cleaning more stray glass from the broken windows that had fallen inside, I tried the engine. It started. The hood was creased, and the driver's side window was busted. Sean had made a few hits to the driver's door, and it refused to open. But the passenger and rear door opened and closed. I could enter through the passenger's side until the driver's side was fixed. I dialed the insurance agent.

"Ms. Baxter, sorry to hear about your car. But you dropped the comprehensive coverage for collision and vandalism."

"I did?"

"Yes. We discussed it because the car is over ten years old, and you decided against keeping it."

"Okay." Darn.

"But you have full glass coverage on the windshield. I can have someone out later to replace it."

"So, the driver's side window?"

"Not covered."

"Great." I winced.

"My recommendation is, if you decide to repair the car, get three estimates, and go from there. There is a glass company we work with, and I can send someone out to fix the windshield. You do not have to be there."

"Thanks. I'll think about the rest of the repairs." I knew full well that I would not fix the damage. It wouldn't be worth the price of the car.

I went outside to the vehicle and considered the wreckage. Wayne walked up behind me.

"Looks bad."

"It's not pretty. But it runs. The insurance will cover the windshield, but nothing else."

"Yeah, sounds about right." He grunted. "Sorry."

"It's just a car," and I shrugged.

"That's right. It is." He crossed his arms, his brow furrowed. "If you put clear plastic across the driver's side window and get the hood hammered out, you can get by with having the windshield fixed. 'Til you get somethin' better? I might get the hood to latch."

"That'll work." I nodded. "Could you try?"

"I'll give it a whirl." He went to Matilda and got a small rubber mallet. He hammered the end of the hood, bending the metal so that it latched. "Might want to tie it down. It'll stay better."

"I'll get a rope." Digging through my bucket of supplies in the back of the car, I found a short length of rope used previously for tying down loads. He secured the hood and latch and tested it by tugging the edge of the hood.

"Should work." He nodded.

"Thanks Wayne."

"No problem."

"I have one more favor to ask?"

"What's that?" He brushed his ponytail back and gazed at me.

"Not a word of this to the sheriff." I put a finger to my lips.

"You sure? He might get you a new car?" He peered over his lenses, his brows up. "You're set to get married?"

"Don't want to talk about it." I bit my bottom lip and avoided his perplexed stare.

"All righty, then." He squinted at the SUV, then asked with a sideways glance. "Want to hitch a ride with me to the rehab?"

"Absolutely, positively yes. Thanks." I grinned. "I'll get my bag."

***

On the drive to the renovation, I asked, "How is Gretta doing with her insomnia?"

"Sleepwalking seems done. The counselor she's seeing is getting through to her."

"That's good." I nodded.

"She's remembering promises she and Walter made to each other." He glanced at me.

"Like what?" I tilted my head and waited. He parked in the driveway of the house. Pausing our conversation, we studied the front. The garage looked intact. Sean hadn't taken another go at the house. Relieved, we piled out of Wayne's work van. I opened the house, and we trooped in.

Inside, Wayne continued, "They said they were soul mates. They promised each other they wouldn't remarry when one of them passed."

"Okay?" Puzzled, I studied Wayne in the foyer's light. "Gretta promised Walter she wouldn't ever remarry? Walter agreed to that, too?"

"He was a character. Gretta says he was a big man, had a big personality." Wayne paused, his head tilted, and he rubbed his chin. "She said he promised he would become a hermit, a monk, if he outlived her. He loved her."

"Monkshood! That explains it! That was the plant she supposedly used to kill Walter. She felt guilty about breaking her end of the deal by getting married again."

"The mind can play tricks on you. I figure it got all twisted in her head, and it came out in her sleepwalking and falsely confessing."

"Makes sense," I said.

"Course she didn't plan on meeting a fella like me." He flipped his ponytail back and grinned. "I'm a good catch. She is too!"

"Yes. You two are perfect together. I am sure Gretta and Walter meant it at the time, but things change. She should not feel guilty about remarrying. If Walter truly loved her, he would want her to be happy."

"Thanks, I needed that." He let out a breath.

"No problem." I studied him. "This has been tough for both of you."

"Yep. But it's working itself out. We're good." He grinned.

"I'm glad." I nodded. My cell rang, and I reached for it, checking the caller info. It was the windshield replacement company. "I have to get this."

"I'll get started on the new mantel." He went into the garage.

"We're finished replacing the windshield on your SUV," the young technician who identified himself as Rocky said. "Looks like there's another broken window and some damage?"

"I'll take care of it. The car still runs."

"Okay. Thank you for your business. I will leave the paperwork with the vehicle."

"Sure." I clicked off. I quelled the thought that Sean could come back and take another go at the SUV while it was in the parking lot. I hadn't moved the car to its garage stall. I muttered to myself, "He's got to work sometime," and banished that thought while I surveyed my to-do list.

Chapter 29

I headed to the basement with a can of gray paint for the floor. Now that I knew the blood samples had been collected, I could go ahead with washing down the surfaces and painting. I flipped on the radio to country rock while I wiped the back of the water softener and thought about my conversation with Wayne.

Jake and I believed we were soul mates. Had I promised I wouldn't remarry if something happened to him? We hadn't had enough time. Life had changed in a nanosecond after he died, saving a kid from an oncoming train. Did Don's job scare me? I groaned. Yeah, it did. We had talked about it, but I'd kept my feelings in check. Jake's accident was a fluke. People have accidents, professions aside. Don had stayed out of harm's way thus far, and fingers crossed, he would continue to stay safe.

My phone rang, sounding in my jeans pocket, while I wrapped up the cleaning. I turned the radio down and plucked out the phone. I stared at the CID, Penelope Young.

"Hello?" I answered, not sure if this was a joke, or if Sean was using her phone.

"I am calling for Katelyn Baxter," a soft voice came.

"This is she."

"My name is Penelope. My husband is Sean Young."

"Yes. I know who you are." You are married to a suspected murderer.

"I am calling to warn you. My husband is a very angry man, and he is furious with you. You must be careful. I am afraid of what he could do."

"He's already bashed my car and smashed the garage of the house he sold me."

"Property damage is a small thing. He can do much worse."

I waited, dread churning in my stomach.

"Why are you calling me? You should tell the police what you know."

"I am too afraid."

"They can protect you," I urged.

"I do not believe that."

"Why not?" I asked.

"I have called them. When he cut down the neighbor's tree, when he snatched off my glasses and broke them."

"I found the glasses! Black frames with rhinestones?"

"Yes. They were mine."

"Did you bleed anywhere?" I asked.

"Yes. When he grabbed my glasses, I lost my balance, landed against a stud, and caught my arm on a nail."

"You reported it to the police?"

"Yes, I did. But he can be charming. I did not think the police believed me, and I didn't want to press charges. I wanted him to stop."

"Uh, huh." That was grim, but now I knew the dried blood was hers, and that Sean wasn't very thorough when he cleaned.

"I was naïve. He cried and said it would never happen again. I believed him."

"What has changed?" I asked.

"I was with him when he smashed your car. It was unreal. His anger was palpable. It was like he was a different person."

"I'm sorry you saw that. Tell the cops you were a witness to the vandalism."

"Again, I am too frightened. He could turn on me."

"He has. You just said he broke your glasses. You fell and hurt yourself."

"Yes. But he has done nothing to me since then. He was angry about the water in the basement. I said something stupid. It was not his fault."

"You can't blame yourself for his temper."

"He is under a lot of pressure. He had to get another job. They think he killed Arthur Cook."

"Did he?" I held my breath, waiting for her answer.

After a long pause, she whispered, "There is evidence in the house. I must go." She clicked off.

I looked at the phone.

"Dang it." Impatiently, I dialed her number. It rang once and went to voicemail, and I hung up. Penelope lost no time in blocking my call and probably deleted any trace of her outgoing call. She must be terrified Sean would get her phone and track her calls. It made sense for her to delete and block.

Rattled, I gazed around the utility room, shaking my head. I'd found keys, the gun, blood. What could be there the police didn't know about? The blood upstairs had proven to be his, and she said the basement blood was hers.

Now that the basement floor was clean and dry, I could paint. But with my nerves shot, I went upstairs to check on Wayne's progress.

"Looks good!" Wayne had cut the new mantel and was sanding, preparing it for stain.

"Yep. You want me to stain it?" he asked.

"Yes. Go ahead." I enjoyed staining and painting, but with the first mantel broken, I could pass on a second time. I left Wayne to do the staining and went back inside.

When Myra called, I was strolling through the house, studying the rooms, trying to figure out what Penelope was telling me. What evidence, where? And why was Penelope telling me? Was she involved in the murder with Sean, either after the fact or part of the deed? Was she trying to distract attention from her?

"I talked to Bernie again," she said.

"What did he say?"

"He said, if we thought our auras combined or Gabriella had cursed us by giving us the same reading, there were a few things we could try before calling a professional to remove the curse." I groaned at the idea of paying someone to remove bad juju.

"Like what?"

"We could try to undo the curse by cleansing ourselves with a sage ritual or taking a salt bath." Burning sage was our go-to for cleansing for all my flips because there seemed to be a negative energy, i.e. dead body, attached to all of them.

"Sounds promising. What's a salt bath?"

"I will bring the instructions for the bath. We can try that on our own."

"Sage sounds good." Soaking in a tub definitely sounded like a solo experience.

She sounded elated, "If that doesn't work, Bernie can remove negative vibes. For a fee."

"I am ready for a cleansing, Myra. You would not believe the day I had yesterday, or who called me today." I blurted, "Penelope! She claims there is evidence in the house."

"Of the murder? You are kidding. How about I bring the wine and sage tonight? And dinner?"

"Wonderful! The sooner, the better." I hung up, happy to have a diversion to look forward to that evening and went to paint the basement floor. By the time I finished, it was time to pack out. I cleaned up the brush and tossed the roller pad. Giving Don a quick call, I said, "Myra's coming over later, so don't worry about me and Boots tonight."

After some hesitation, he said, "If Myra's there, I guess you will be okay. I have to work late at the office tonight."

"All right." I wanted to ask if he would work late with Morgan but didn't. I need to work on those trust issues.

"I'm training Morgan on some new procedures."

"Sure." I felt my shoulders tighten. Procedures. So much for trust.

"How's the car?"

"The windshield's fixed. I'd better go. Wayne's waiting," I said in a rush.

"That is progress. What about the bodywork?"

"Gotta go," I said, and clicked off.

Chapter 30

The first thing I did when we got home was to move my car to its garage stall, out of the path of any attackers wielding iron bars. Tucked safely in the garage, I taped a piece of clear vinyl from a painter's drop cloth over the driver's side window. Sitting in the driver's seat, I looked out of the side window. Okay, not the best, but safe from rain and elements, even if it had a foggy appearance. The new windshield looked great. Satisfied, I climbed out through the passenger's side, went to my place, fed Boots, and got cleaned up for Myra's visit.

"I have all your favorites," Myra announced. "Hawaiian pizza, Chardonnay, and sage, lavender candle, and a feather for each of us." She placed the pizza on my counter, took out the sage and candle from her tote bag, and added that to the bounty. From an inside pocket of the tote, she brought out two large white feathers and held them up.

"Feathers?"

"Bernie said to use the feather to waft the smoke from the lit sage over our bodies to eliminate any negative energy."

She brought out a sheet of paper from the pocket of her designer jacket, and said, "The directions for a salt bath. You might want to double up on curse removals."

"I'll do whatever it takes," I deadpanned.

"That bad?"

"Myra, my car looks like it has been through a tornado. Sean beat the heck out of it. Penelope called me today to warn me he was furious with me."

"You've been busy." She frowned. "Let's eat while we talk."

"I am famished. Thanks for the goodies!" I left the bath instructions on the counter, took out plates, and we helped ourselves to pizza and wine, settling in the living room.

"What happened with the car?" Myra asked. Between bites of heavenly sweet and spicey pizza, I said, "I got the bug to see if I could talk to Penelope at Maxim's. But Sean picked her up from work and must have seen me lurking. Because after I got home from my surveillance, he took a tire iron to my car. Wayne and Gretta saw them. Then today, out of the blue, she calls to warn me, like I needed warning." I shook my head and groaned. "She said there was evidence in the house. She could have had a part in the murder?"

"It's hard to know what is up with her. She was in the car with Sean when he was beating on your car. She was scared and could be a victim of her husband's temper."

"That's likely it." I nodded. "She sounded stressed when she hung up."

"Your imagination is on overload," Myra said.

"My paranoia." I laughed.

"I think we need to do the sage first. You have a negative streak going."

"You think?" I laughed and took our dirty dishes to the kitchen. Then I retrieved the sage, candle, and feathers, and placed them on the coffee table. By now, we were old hands with the ritual, and I lit the candle, placed the sage on a plate, and handed Myra a feather. The feathers were a new feature.

"Remember your intention," she said.

"Yes." I closed my eyes, feather in hand, visualizing a serene outcome for my love life, flip, and any other chaos in my life. "Curse, be gone. Back to where you came from." Opening my eyes, I brought the plate of sage over my face and body, waving the feather to spread the smoke. Coughing lightly, I handed the sage to Myra, "Your turn." She followed suit with her intention for the curse to leave.

"What do you think?" I asked. Then I jumped, spooked by a knock at the door.

Myra gasped; her eyes widened. "Are you expecting anyone?"

"No." Quickly, I put the feather aside and went to the door, peering through the security hole. "It's Eddy. Should I let him in?"

"I can hear you." Eddy said from the hall. Myra snickered and blew out the lavender scented candle.

"Is there any pizza left?" she asked. I nodded.

"I heard you too, Myra," Eddy called, his voice muffled.

I chuckled and opened the door. "What are you doing here?"

"Pizza?" He sniffed the air and grinned.

I swore he had a sixth sense when it came to food.

"Come in." I waved him in and closed the door. "I'll get you some pizza."

"Great," he smiled happily. "Any beer?" He settled into the couch next to Myra. Boots came over to sniff him and nuzzle his legs.

"No. Chardonnay."

"Wine's good." He nodded.

"You didn't say why you were here?" There were a couple of slices of pizza left, and I fixed a plate and a glass of wine.

"Just driving by, thought I'd stop and say hi."

"How's the new job?" I asked, fearing the worst.

"Job's good." He nodded.

"And Lola?"

"I'm back in the house." He grinned.

Myra and I looked at one another and we snickered.

"So, what's up with the sage?" Eddy saw my plate of the scorched herb and the candle. I palmed the feather and slipped it into the tote, and Myra folded hers in her lap out of view.

"I should go," Myra said and got to her feet.

"Don't leave on account of me," Eddy protested.

"No, it's getting late," she said and went for her jacket.

Another knock came.

Frowning, I peered through the security hole, then opened the door. "Don?"

"Hey Katelyn, I was worried about your being here after what happened with your car." He spied Eddy in the easy chair, eating pizza. "Hey Eddy?" Eddy held his plate up in greeting and sipped his wine. Don pursed his lips. "Didn't know there was a party."

"No party," I said.

"I was just leaving, Don. Good to see you again," Myra said. Stepping around him, she nodded at Eddy and waved goodbye.

"Say 'hi' to your brother for me." Don smiled and nodded.

"I will. Good night, all," Myra left. Don focused on Eddy, who drank the last of his wine and stood.

"Something happen to your car, Katie?" Eddy asked.

"Long story, for another time," I said.

"Sure. I'll take off too. Thanks for the food." He threw his arms around me in a hug. "Hope the sage works for you." I gave an eyeroll, then closed my eyes. *Was it necessary for you to say that in front of my fiancé, and hug me, too?*

"I'm sorry if I interrupted anything." Don cleared his throat. "I knew Myra was here, but I'm worried about Sean being out there, now that he knows where you live."

"Yeah, about that. Can't you arrest him for anything? Assaulting a car with a deadly weapon or plain old vandalism?"

"We're working on it. Like I've said before, it is a property crime, not our highest priority. Any pizza left?" He sniffed the air.

"Sorry, no. Eddy finished it."

He gazed at me. Oops.

"I didn't know he would stop by. I didn't know you would stop by," I babbled.

"It's all good. I know you and your ex are friends. You had a history before me. And Eddy is a friendly guy." His blue eyes twinkled as they brushed over my face, which I could feel was turning red with embarrassment.

"Thank you for understanding. Eddy is just Eddy."

"Uh huh, how about you and Boots come and stay with me tonight?"

"How about you stay here tonight?" Spreading my arms toward my small living room, which paled in comparison to his digs. "There's the spare room?"

"I thought you'd never ask." He grinned.

Chapter 31

I drove my battered SUV to the job site the next morning, warmed by memories of the evening before. We had talked until all hours, and I sleepily sent him off with a strong cup of coffee and a hard-boiled egg, deciding that Esther was correct. Protein was an important start to the day.

"I'm a Danish pastry guy," but he ate the egg and took a to-go mug of coffee and kissed me on the cheek. "Later."

Wayne was varnishing the mantel in the garage, and the acrid smell permeated the air. It was warming up outside, and I opened the overhead door to let the fresh air in.

"That stuff will kill you," I commented.

"Yep, should have opened it earlier." He grinned.

"It looks good." I viewed the piece. "We will be in business soon. After the mantel is installed, there isn't much to do before the house goes on the market. Final clean-up, a cleansing to rid the house of Sean's bad juju, and staging."

"Yep, should be good. Saw the lawman's car in the lot last night," he chuckled. "Glad to have police protection with that guy, Sean, on the loose."

"It was like grand central station with Myra, Eddy, and Don." I yawned. "Could have had you and Gretta over, too."

"We were bushed, had an early night. Any news about the car attacker?" He nodded toward the sad sight of my Ford in the driveway.

"No." I looked out at the street and saw a pickup truck slow and park at the curb. "Eddy, so soon?"

"Hey, Katie," Eddy stepped out of his truck. "Sorry, kind of ate and ran last night." He circled my car, his brows raised. "Hope the other guy's car looks worse?"

"Yeah, and it won't be the last time I tick off somebody. Shouldn't you be at work?"

"Hey Eddy," Wayne called.

"Wayne," he nodded. "Early lunch."

Shrugging, he headed to the garage. "I can fix the side mirror and driver's window. It may not be pretty, but it'll be safer."

"How much?"

"Let's call it even for favors extended. I'll get parts from the local salvage yard."

"Sounds good. Go for it."

"Kiddo, think I'll get an early lunch too. While this piece is drying." Wayne had finished varnishing and removed yellow rubber gloves that snapped as he pulled them off. He patted his shirt pocket where he kept his cigarettes. "Need smokes, too. I'll be back."

"Hot dog at the gas station?"

"Yep." He grinned and went to his van.

"So, this is the new place?" Eddy looked around and whistled. "Nice. What's the price on it?"

"Are you in the market?" I asked, my head tilted, following Eddy's gaze around the garage.

"Lola isn't happy with the Bluebird house." He quickly glanced at me, then feigned interest in the pegboard that once held tools.

"She isn't?" My stomach dipped at the thought of finding another renter.

"Nope." He walked the depth of the garage. "This is a big space. A guy could do a lot of stuff in here. Carpentry, fix cars, still have room to park a car." He stooped over and reached into a corner beside a wall stud. "What's this?" He picked up a piece of metal from part of the garage where I hadn't swept yet.

"Don't know." I frowned.

He held up the metal. "It's a gun shell casing."

My stomach dropped. "Evidence." Stunned, I said, "I'll get a bag." Not wanting to add my prints to the casing, I headed to my car and snagged an empty fast-food bag. "I'll call the police."

***

I was relieved to see Morgan Clark drive up and park behind my car. I didn't want to ruin the time I'd had with Don the evening earlier with another conversation about a possible murder in the house I was rehabbing. She got out, her narrow-set eyes viewing my wreck.

"Are you driving this vehicle?" she asked, poised to write a ticket.

"Not at the moment," I said, my hands stuffed in the pocket of my jeans, fingers crossed. It was true. At that moment, I was not behind the wheel, with the engine running, and gears engaged.

"You reported a spent shell casing at this location?" she asked. "Possible evidence?"

"Yes." I handed her the bag. "In here."

"Where was it found?"

"In that corner," I pointed to the area where Eddy had spied the casing.

"Uh, huh." She kneeled and focused her flashlight under the framing. Scooting along the corner and wall, she straightened. "Anything else?"

"No. But I haven't finished cleaning the garage."

"It's possible we missed it during our searches, but not likely." She stood and stared pointedly. "Who has access to this garage?"

I blinked. "A lot of people, my carpenter, Wayne, the garage door installer, the investigators after the driver smashed the front of the garage. Anyone walking by could have undone the tarp and entered. It wasn't locked until the new door was installed with a new security code. Eddy here," I nodded toward him, "just spotted the casing."

"This appears suspicious." Morgan's eyes drilled into mine.

"Gotta get back to work, Kate." Eddy said. "I'll check with you later," he said and winked. "I found the casing, but that's all I know," he said and held up his hands. "And I'm on lunch."

"I'll need your name and contact number before you can go," Morgan said.

"Yes, ma'am. Thank you." Eddy smiled, his brown eyes sparkling charm, his tone polite. He wrote his information on a pad Morgan proffered, and left.

"I found a gun in the mantel. It is a three fifty-seven Smith and Wesson?" My knowledge of guns was marginal, preferring to leave that to professionals. "Sheriff Don took the weapon."

"This shell casing couldn't have come from that gun." Morgan slipped on rubber gloves she took from her police car. "This casing is from a semi-automatic pistol. The Smith and Wesson doesn't leave casings."

"All right." I nodded.

"I'll give it to ballistics, check to see if there's a match to what we have."

"Great."

"Seems suspicious that it shows up now and that the investigators didn't find it." She studied me and sniffed. "You wouldn't want to conceal evidence in a murder case. So you can sell this house with no murder attached to it?"

"I just now found it! In fact, it wasn't me, it was my-ex-husband, Eddy, who found it."

"Aren't you engaged to Sheriff Williams?" Her brows rose, and she peered at me.

"Yes." I knew it was a rhetorical question. She knew we were engaged and was making some kind of dig. I kept my expression neutral.

"And your EX found the casing?" she asked.

"It's complicated," I added, defensively. "Sheriff Williams knows everything there is to know about Eddy. It is no secret."

"Uh, huh. The department will be in touch." Morgan Clark stomped back to her police car and sped off. The relief I had had in seeing the deputy instead of Don was short-lived.

Dottie trotted across the lawns to where I stood, my arms crossed, watching Morgan's hasty departure.

"So, the police were here?" She looked guilty, adding, "I couldn't help but see the cruiser. I was filling the bird feeders. Well, they're more squirrel feeders than bird," she giggled. "But I noticed the car?"

"Yes. Dottie." I was glum about Morgan's accusations and wasn't feeling very sociable. She wore a tote slung over her shoulder; inside, a bag of birdseed was visible from where I stood.

"It sounded like they found an object?"

"Yes. My ex found a spent gun casing in the garage."

"Isn't that something? The papers said Arthur had been shot. Your ex found a casing? Do you mean ex-husband?" The stocky woman looked at me curiously.

"Yes. We are friends, nothing more," I said firmly.

"Of course," she amended. My face was stoney, and she backed away. "Well, I will get back to my feeders. The front of the garage looks great. Good to see you again. Have a nice day."

I nodded and went into the garage. Wayne returned from his lunch, satisfied after his visit to the gas station. The scent of cigarette smoke clung to his clothing. He did a light sanding on the mantel before adding another coat of varnish. He looked happy. I didn't have the heart to tell him about the shell casing or my visit from Morgan. He had enough stress with Gretta.

I called Don, unhappy about Morgan's visit.

"You and Morgan haven't hit it off," Don said.

"She insinuated I was withholding evidence. On top of not giving you my messages."

"She gives me your messages, but she could be more prompt," he said mildly.

"Whatever." I huffed.

"Do you mind if I stop by this evening?"

"You think I still need protection?"

"It couldn't hurt," he said. "I'll bring dinner, and there's some paperwork we need to go over."

"Paperwork?"

"How about I pick up Chinese food and a nice bottle of red wine?"

"What paperwork?"

"I'll be there about six o'clock."

I had time to feed Boots and shower. Then I slipped on a soft blue sweater with my good blue jeans and pulled back my damp hair in a scrunchie. Feeling revived, I slapped on lip gloss.

In a weird cosmic coincidence, we wore the same colors. He had showered and changed and looked like a million bucks. His hair smelled of some kind of woodsy type of shampoo. His jeans fit in all the right places, and his shirt was a deep blue that matched his eyes. He held carryout containers from an oriental food joint, a bottle of wine, and a manilla envelope. I grabbed the containers and wine while he slipped off his jacket and sat at the kitchen table. After putting out dishes and wine glasses, I sat across from him.

"Let's eat first." He rose and left the manilla envelope in the living room, then returned to the kitchen.

"Sure." My brows furrowed, following his actions.

"Have you thought of a time and place for the wedding?" he asked, as we dug into the food.

"Not yet." I gulped.

"How about June?"

"June weddings are lovely." Idly, I pushed the food around on my plate and reached for my wineglass and took a large drink.

"Your house should be finished?"

"Finished and sold, I hope."

"It would be a good time for a fresh start. We can move you and Boots into my house."

I tensed and plunged ahead. "It would be best if we found a new place for us. For a fresh start."

"You really don't like my house?" he asked. Sitting back, he studied me.

"Your house is your house. I want us to have *our* house," I said.

"All right." He reached for my hand. "We will look for a new house. But I want to go ahead with the wedding. It will take time to find a home we both like."

"I would like a timeline for the house. I wouldn't want to move twice."

"I see what you mean. Let's start looking."

"Yes, let's do that." I nodded. It was becoming all too real, and I felt rushed.

He got up and cleared the dishes, then went for the envelope and opened it.

"My lawyer thought it was best we get this out of the way, too." He slipped out a sheaf of papers and placed the document in front of me.

"What is this?" I read the title, "Minnesota Prenuptial Agreement. Are you kidding me?"

"Now, Katelyn," he said, his voice calm and collected. Too calm.

"No." My blood pressure felt as if it had risen 50 points.

"My lawyer thought because of the difference in our assets, it would be best if we had an agreement going into marriage."

"Then marry your lawyer!" I stood up. "If you do not trust me, then this marriage is doomed from the start."

"Now, Katelyn," he repeated in the same infuriatingly calm voice. "Let's talk about this."

"We have talked. The answer is no. Go!" I pointed to the door. When he sat there, not moving, staring at me, I hurried to the door, and waited while he gathered the paperwork and his coat.

He stopped in the doorway.

"Katelyn, be reasonable," he said, with a raised hand.

I pushed him the rest of the way out and slammed the door behind him. Frustrated, I slipped off the engagement ring and put it back in its case, leaving it in my bedside drawer.

Chapter 32

It was Friday morning, and I had given Wayne the day off when we left the house the day before. I hoped he and Gretta could unwind over the long weekend. Unable to sleep after the furor with Don, I headed to the rehab at an ungodly hour to work. After cleaning the rest of the garage, I called Myra.

"It's not unusual that someone who has a lot of assets wants to protect them," Myra said.

"Then he should not get married. Live with, and love, his assets," I snarked. "He has shown he didn't trust me from the get-go. Remember how we found out about his mansion via the internet? We didn't know if it was real, or if it was the same person. Finally, I had to say something!"

"He could have been burned in an earlier relationship?" she asked. "You said he didn't want his wealth to be a 'thing.' Something that divides the two of you. Remember the con job that Robin Steele did on him?"

"I do. We've all been burned at some time or another. Look at Eddy. I am over it. Besides, Don's never told me anything like that."

"Yes, but would you commit to Eddy again?"

"No. Lesson learned."

"Maybe Don isn't so sure of that."

"What?" I frowned.

"Being the devil's advocate, suppose you marry Don. You two are going through a rough patch. Eddy shows up and swoops you away. There is no prenup. You get half of Don's assets or whatever the lawyers agree on."

"Believe me, there's no swooping with Eddy."

"You danced with him," she said. "At Ivan's."

"I swayed. It is not the same." Sometimes, I hated that Myra, although she was a good confidant, had the memory of an elephant, and reminded me of what had happened at Ivan's the night Eddy got his newest job.

"Myra, I don't think that's it. We have had the conversation about Eddy. He is a friend. I think Don has more confidence in himself than that."

"I'm just saying. You and Eddy have a past."

"I'm hanging up now." I disconnected, and frustrated, ran my hands through my hair. Standing in the rehab's kitchen, I surveyed the progress. Myra had a good point about the disparity between Don's and my assets. If the situation was reversed and I was wealthy, would I want a prenup? I shook my head, no, I would not. Eddy and I had lean times and better times, but it was his straying that led to our break-up. Well, that and our hot tempers and his lost jobs.

I had a good marriage with Jake, and that did a lot to mend my confidence. If I wanted a prenup, it would not be because of money. It would mean I had reservations about the person I was committing to. But rich people are different. He had to have learned that 'protect your money' from growing up in a family that had money, their car dealership.

Was I too friendly with Eddy? I didn't think so. I didn't think Don thought so. But there was a little niggle about that evening at Ivan's. We had swayed to the music, and I had drunk too much wine.

"It's time I had that salt bath." With that in mind, I closed the rehab, satisfied with the day's progress, and headed to my car. Absorbed with my thoughts, Dottie's voice intruded as she trotted across the lawns that separated the houses.

"So, have the police said anything about the gun casing?" she asked, breathless from her hike.

"They haven't had it long enough. It takes time for ballistics, and they won't tell me anything, anyway."

Dottie's face fell.

"If it has anything to do with a crime, it's policy not to divulge anything about an ongoing investigation," I said.

"Sure, I was just wondering." Her expression was bland, her bubbly personality dimmed.

"Is something troubling you, Dottie?" My senses were on high alert, viewing her demeanor. "You can tell me."

"Well," she cleared her throat. "It's been bothering me." And she rushed on, "I only put the shell casing in your garage because Penelope asked me to. She was afraid they weren't getting any closer to solving Arthur's murder."

"You put the shell casing in the garage?" I gasped. "You planted evidence? When?"

"Before you fixed the door, I snuck in overnight and left it. And it wasn't like that. Penelope is so unhappy with Sean." She whispered, "She doesn't know how she can leave."

"Except to have Sean arrested? Where did she get the casing from?"

"She didn't say. She just said it was important."

"Dottie, talk to the police. Tell them what Penelope told you."

"I am afraid Sean will come after me. He knows Penelope and I talk. He is very jealous and controlling."

I had to consider her view. If Sean could beat on my car, what could he do to Dottie, a nosy neighbor, me, or Penelope? What had he done? Given my present situation with Don, I squelched my impulse to call him. Dottie would have to contact the authorities. Don and I were at an impasse.

"It sounds like you and Penelope talked a lot while they lived here?"

"I liked her. We would chat. She trusted me."

"Did she ever talk about Arthur?"

"She thought she was in love with him," Dottie said, hesitant. "She said it 'just' happened while she was temping at Maxim's. He would pay attention to her. She was planning to leave Sean when Arthur was killed."

"Did she ever say anything about how Arthur felt about her?" Dottie shifted and avoided my gaze. Reluctantly, she said, "From what Penelope said, I gathered he seemed less smitten, if you know what I mean?"

"How so?"

"Once he got the promotion, he could have arranged for Human Resources to give her a permanent position. He didn't."

"But that would have been a conflict with HR if Sean still worked in the same area. Spouses working in the same department."

"He could have found her a position somewhere in the company," she said stubbornly.

"She didn't want to teach?"

"She was losing faith in finding a permanent teaching position, and she was tired of being a substitute teacher. You remember how it was when we went to school?"

"Substitute teachers got the most grief." I nodded and chuckled.

"Besides, she wanted to be close to Arthur. She loved him even when he left her hanging."

"So, she waited for Arthur?"

"He would break dates, tell her a 'thing' came up, and she would go through all sorts of emotions. She was on a high, then a low." Clearing her throat, she studied the ground. "I always thought he had other interests. A fiancé being one, and the rumors there were other women." Dottie raised her head and held my gaze. "But Penelope couldn't see that."

"I'd heard he was engaged," I said. "Penelope had to have known that?"

"She didn't believe it. She thought it was a rumor to hide their relationship from Sean and everyone at the company."

"Really?" I was nonplussed.

That fit with what I had heard about Arthur Brett Cook's character. He was a player. If Penelope wanted out of a bad marriage and found out Arthur had 'other interests,' could she have murdered him? Was the "evidence" hidden in the house really meant to steer investigators away from her? I had to find Arthur's fiancé. She could have done in Arthur if she found out he was a philanderer.

"Dottie, I need to go. There is a bath waiting for me." I had to dispel the negativity that surrounded me with this house, Don's prenup bid, and now Dottie's confession about planting evidence. And learning more about her tight relationship with Penelope.

"You look beat, Katelyn. I love a nice long soak. My favorite is that lavender-scented bubble bath. You can get it almost anywhere." Her buoyant personality returned while I crawled in through the passenger's door, over the console, and got behind the wheel. She was still waving as I reached the street and headed home.

Chapter 33

The directions Myra had left for the salt bath were simple: Epsom or Himalayan salt with baking soda. An essential oil was optional. Say a mantra for removing any negativity before you enter the bath, and soak for 30-40 minutes. I lit a candle for extra negativity removal, recited a spell, and soaked. My Epsom salt was the foaming bubble bath kind, and I felt my worries melt away and closed my eyes. Boots was very curious about the whole cast out negativity ritual and wandered in and out while I soaked.

My eyes flew open when I heard a knock at my door. Boots sat in the doorway while I debated about whether to answer.

"Katelyn! Are you there?" It was Don's voice. I waited, leisurely dipping under the water. It had been about a twenty-minute soak in the tub. More knocking. I lingered in the bath water.

"I fired my lawyer! I'm sorry!"

Snatching up a towel, I dried off and yelled, "Coming!" Dressing in my robe and wrapping my wet hair with a towel, I yelled, "Apology accepted!" and threw open the door to Don, who wore his work uniform.

Boots weaved around us while we hugged. After a long embrace, he said, "Let's get you and Boots packed up and go to my place."

"It's your weekend to stay here," I said, scrunching my face.

"Is it? I don't know, I've lost track."

"Me too. Let's go to your place." He had Esther, and Sean hadn't found his way to Don's home, like he had mine. Safety first. "I'll get packed." My heart sang while I dried my hair and dressed and packed a weekend bag.

***

Esther was in fine form as she greeted us at the entry to Don's elegant home.

"There is a beef roast in the oven, with potatoes and carrots, and it will be done at seven o'clock. If it is okay, I will leave for the weekend for my sister's house," she said.

"Yes, Esther. Katelyn and I can manage. Enjoy your weekend."

"Thank you. I will see you on Monday." She smiled and took her coat from the entry closet.

I inhaled the aroma of the roast beef, my mouth watering. The stress of the prenup had dampened any urge for food and I had skipped lunch, surviving on coffee and a handful of nuts. I had chucked the Chinese leftovers in a fit of exasperation.

"You and Boots get settled. I'll take a shower and change; see you downstairs?" His eyes caressed my face, and he smiled as he left me in the hallway between the suites.

"Sounds good." Boots scampered to the window and jumped to the cat tower, his tail swishing while he looked out. He made a low, guttural noise, and I went to the window. Parked in the circular drive below, there was a blue vehicle waiting.

"No! It can't be." I exhaled, relieved, and chuckled as Esther opened the passenger's side and got in. "Boots, you had me worried. It's Esther leaving. That must be her sister."

I unpacked and headed to the kitchen to check on the roast. Esther had thought of everything. She had set the table with fine dishes, crystal stemware, and silver. The dinner was a celebration of sorts, and I found an open bottle of wine on the counter with two glasses.

Boots had followed me downstairs, and I took his chow from my tote and fed him. While I waited for Don, I poured a glass of wine, started the gas fireplace, and settled in the great room of the spacious mansion. The room was furnished with a rich brown leather sectional, traditional wood tables, and brass lamps. It was decidedly masculine. My taste could be described as eclectic, with touches of traditional, contemporary bookshelves, and thrift store finds. It would be a challenge to meld our tastes.

"Let's eat! I am famished." Don's voice made me jump.

"Yes!"

We headed to the kitchen, taking our plates from the dining room, served ourselves in the kitchen, and seated ourselves back in the dining room.

"You have a beautiful home, and Esther makes a mean pot roast."

"I do, and she does," Don said, his eyes lighting up. I felt a twinge of guilt at my insistence that we have a fresh start with a home of our choosing. He put down his fork. "I didn't mean to blindside you with the prenup."

Now I felt guilty. Okay. Not that guilty.

"So, you're good with no prenup?" I asked, focused on his big blues.

"I am."

"And finding a home that would be ours together?"

"I like my home," he said.

My eyebrows raised, and he hurriedly said, "But a home on the lake would be acceptable." I held my stare,

"To start a new life together." Relaxing, I held up my glass, and he held up his and met my gaze.

"You're one tough lady," he said.

"You're no slouch either," I said with a grin.

Chapter 34

We retired to the great room with another glass of wine and watched the flames of the fireplace, wrapped in each other's arms.

"I had a conversation with the neighbor, Dottie. I thought you might find it interesting." Clearing my throat, I sat up.

"Do we have to talk about your renovations?"

"It's my job."

"I suppose. What did she say?" He sat up and draped his arm around me, and we leaned back.

"She said she put the spent gun casing in the garage of the rehab. She said Penelope asked her to."

He stiffened and withdrew his arm. Rubbing his head, he said, "The casing Morgan picked up." He sighed heavily. "Now, you're telling me. Did she say why?"

"I know, I should have told you right away." Wincing with an apology, I said, "Penelope told her that it was important."

"So, Dottie compromised an ongoing investigation. And Penelope asked her to."

"She said she did it for Penelope. She is scared, and they haven't arrested Sean. And Sean seems to get away with a lot of mischief, and maybe even murder."

"Katelyn, we can't discuss this." He placed a finger on my lips to silence me. "If Dottie has information or evidence about Arthur's murder, she needs to talk to the investigator."

"I told her that."

"Good. We are done, then. No more talking about murder."

My cellphone rang, and I frowned. It was on, but tucked away in my bag.

"Who would call?" I looked at Don. He shrugged. "Go ahead, answer it."

I retrieved the phone from my purse by the end table and checked the display.

"It's Wayne."

"Kiddo, there's a problem here. Sorry to call. You at the lawman's place?"

"Yes. What is it?" It wasn't like Wayne to call at night.

"It's Eddy."

"What about Eddy?" My shoulders tensed.

"I've got my door cracked, watching some guy outside of your door, yelling for you to come out. I'll put it on speakerphone."

"But Eddy is inside my place?" I asked, trying to make sense of the commotion coming from Wayne's call.

Gretta's high-pitched voice came, "He's kicking in the door."

Eddy's voice boomed, "What the hell's with you, man!"

"Call 9-1-1!" I yelled.

"I did!" There were sirens in the background, and I heard Wayne shutting a door. "I think he's gone now. Eddy scared him off."

"Is Eddy there now?" I heard Wayne open the door.

"He's talking to the cops in the hall." His voice was hushed.

"I'm coming home." I hung up. Don was up, his jacket on, and ready to go.

"Are you okay to drive?" I asked.

"Yes."

"I'll get my stuff."

"No, we're coming back here," he insisted. "You'll be safer."

Don had taken out the Corvette with the warmer spring temperatures. And although it wasn't my favorite car, he drove expertly and speedily, and I closed my eyes, clutching the shoulder strap as he maneuvered Friday night traffic on the freeway back to my place. My knees wobbled a little, climbing out of the beast and getting my footing on land.

We entered the townhome hall, and I darted to the door of my unit. The metal door was intact but dented at the bottom. I rushed inside. Eddy had crashed on the sofa.

"Hi Katie," he said.

"Do not 'hi Katie,' me. What happened!"

"Some dude was trying to get in. I scared him off. It's all good. Hey Sheriff."

"Eddy." Don nodded.

"Who was it?" I asked.

"Didn't get his name. He sure looked surprised, though." He chuckled. Don and I looked at each other.

"Did you see what he was driving?" I asked.

"Some kind of van. One taillight was out. Too dark out to see much else. I made a report. Police said they couldn't do anything. Guy was gone."

"Sean Young?"

"Had to be. Doubt Esther would do this." I chuckled, remembering the start I had seeing her sister's vehicle earlier.

"What are you doing here, Eddy?" I asked. "Oh, never mind." I threw up my hands.

"You can't be too rough on him, Kate. He scared the creep away," Don said.

"I guess." I shrugged.

"Let's go," Don said.

"Lock up when you leave, Eddy," I called over my shoulder as we left. Don arched a brow with a wry smile. He opened the passenger's door and then got behind the wheel. Starting the Corvette with a flourish, he gave me a sideways gaze.

"So, that Eddy is a friendly sort of guy. He seems to carry an affection for you?"

I stiffened. Was I missing something about Eddy?

"Eddy has an affection for Eddy," I said. "We're just friends, now."

"Uh, huh. He has a key?" He sped up. I gripped the shoulder strap.

"It's not what it looks like. He probably had a fight with Lola and needed a place to crash." I did not know where, or how, Eddy got another key. But I vowed to find out.

Part of me rebelled at Don's questions.

"We aren't married yet," I spouted. "Eddy's the only family I have besides Myra, Wayne, and Gretta."

He slowed the race car, exiting the freeway smoothly, and the car rumbled along until we reached his home. He hit the remote, opened the gates, pulled into the garage, switched off the engine, and turned to me, "Katelyn, I get it."

"Thank you," I was relieved. We climbed out of the Corvette, and I continued, "He's like the stray relative that shows up for dinner and will help like family does."

"I'm not sure how that will work when we get married," he said, shutting the car door and facing me.

"You'll be my family, too," I said. Grinning, he wrapped his arms around me, and I rested my head against his shoulder. "And Eddy will probably still show up for food."

He roared with laughter. "Okay, we can feed him from time to time." We walked hand in hand into the house.

Chapter 35

I spent part of Sunday night updating Myra on my weekend with Don and the chaos at my house on Friday night.

"Negativity appears to have a hold on your life," Myra mused. "So, you said you tried a salt bath? You followed the directions?" Myra's teaching background was on full display.

"My soak was for a shorter length than the directions said, about 20 minutes against the recommended 30-40 minutes," I admitted, scanning the paper.

"At least 30-40 minutes," Myra corrected. "That is it! You need to spend more time soaking."

"I will see where I can fit in a long soak. The rehab is shaping up, but there is always the last-minute stuff to do before the first showing. It gets busy." Secretly, I was doubting the rituals to dispel negativity, but I didn't want to disappoint Myra. And, heck, who was I to say it didn't work, if I hadn't followed the directions to a 't?'

"You sound calmer, less stressed about making the commitment."

"Yes. I think Don understands what Eddy is to me. He is an old friend, that is all."

"So, the partial soak was beneficial," she said firmly. "That's good. How did Eddy get in?"

"I don't know. I took back the last key he had."

Smacking the side of my head, it hit me. I had stashed the key in my glove box, figuring I would have my car close by if I needed the spare house key. The welcome mat hadn't worked, and the ledge over my door was a little risky, not to mention obvious. The hallway that connected the townhomes didn't have a fake plant to hide a key in. That seemed too easy, too. So, it was the car, until I came up with a better idea.

"Myra, let me call you back."

When Don brought me home that day, he had searched the townhouse. He'd gone in ahead of me, his hand at his service gun, and went through each room. I had watched from the hall, feeling queasy that he had to search, but glad he was there. He had left, saying, "I'll be back later."

"It should be okay. Sean won't be back now. He knows a man could be here."

"Eddy," he said, and gave a sigh. "I'll check later."

"Don't worry. Wayne and Gretta are next door. The walls are so thin here, they will hear if anything is amiss."

"Uh, huh." He had locked his deep blues with my brown eyes, hugged me, and left.

I hadn't been to my SUV since coming home, and I trekked across the parking lot to the garages. Surveying the car, the side window and outside mirror had been replaced. The mirror casing was white and did not match the body paint, but it was there. An improvement, and driving would be a lot easier looking through glass again. Eddy, true to his word, had worked on the car. The driver's door was still dented. After trying it, I found it was still not useable.

I went to the passenger's side and checked the glovebox. Rifling through receipts and CDs, I came up empty. Eddy must have used the key I had taped to the back of the compartment. Both the key and tape were gone. I unloaded the contents of the box and sifted through them to be doubly sure he hadn't returned the key.

I dialed Myra.

"Mystery solved, Eddy did some repairs on the car and took my spare key. He must have kept it."

"You should ask him," she countered.

"Yep, you are right. I'd better get going. It is going to be a big week." Sunday nights were planning nights for the week ahead. Sundays were fun days, but the fun was over.

"Sure. Don't forget the salt bath. I must prepare for the electrician again tomorrow morning."

"Okay, Myra. I'll try to fit it in. What is up with the electrician?" She hadn't mentioned him, and he had slipped to the back of my mind with Don and Eddy and the nightmare of Sean Young.

"He's going to quote me for new wiring on the carriage house. I have my list together for him to add more outlets and replace another fixture. May as well have it done at the same time."

"I didn't know you were in the market for more work?" Myra's home on the 'couple's lake' in Minneapolis was a spectacular red-brick colonial with a carefully manicured lawn. The carriage house was a quaint building from the past that housed her slick SUV and separate living quarters for any live-in help or guests.

"I am not. But he insisted on checking the wiring. It couldn't hurt. The electrical is the same age as the house."

"Yes, indeed. Wiring is important." My mind went immediately to the two-story I was flipping. Thank goodness the house was newer, and the electrical was up to date.

"Besides, he brings stellar pastries from that new little cafe, Pastry Palace, in Hiptown."

"Nice!"

"It is. We'll have to go there."

"Excellent idea." I hung up from Myra. She sounded downright blissful. Maybe she would find another man to dance with. She had always been self-sufficient and poo-poohed any romantic interest after her Marvin's death. The reading with Gabriella could have opened a door. Then again, the second part of her reading, as mine had, dealt with danger to money. Could the electrician be a shyster hiding behind baked goods? I shook my head, disappointed with my suspicions. Myra deserved a good man. The electrician could be the one.

Chapter 36

Monday morning, I headed to the rehab with my list of things to do.

A red convertible pulled into the driveway of the rehab. It felt like an electric charge went through me when I spotted Nate Winner behind the wheel of the sports car. The roof was down, and the weather was a perfect spring day for a drive.

"Why do all the hot guys drive sports cars?" I muttered, then smiled, thinking of Don in his vintage Corvette.

"Hi there, I wanted to see the house." He stepped from the car. His blond hair was ruffled from the drive, he wore aviator style sunglasses, and his smile was full-on dazzling.

"You don't have to go to work?" I asked.

"Yes. But I can go in a little late," he said with a casual shrug. "After meeting you, I was curious. We used to hang out here. Thought it'd be fun to see what a rehab specialist does." He winked.

Oh, boy. I gulped. If Nathan Winner was aware of his effect on women, he didn't show it.

"Sure. Come on in." This would be my chance to ask him more about Arthur.

If Arthur, Sean, and Nate all hung out together, he would know if Arthur was engaged. Dottie claimed Arthur was spoken for, but that was through Sean. Penelope didn't buy it. If Arthur was hiding his relationship with Penelope from Sean, what better way to keep any suspicions at bay than to invent a fiancée?

I led the way inside and said, "I don't believe I've changed much of the interior."

"It's a work in process." He squinted. "You're working on the mantel?"

"Yes. Wayne, my carpenter will be here shortly." I took a deep breath and plunged ahead, "So, Arthur was engaged at the time of his death?"

Nate viewed me as he chewed his lower lip. His twinkling eyes held mine. "Maybe he was."

"Maybe?"

"Arthur had a lot of irons in the fire."

"What does that mean?"

"He may have proposed to a woman or two."

"This guy sounds like a scumbag," I said. My cool gaze met Nate's.

He shrugged. "Arthur had power and money. It attracted women. Can't blame a guy for that." He tipped his chin, lazy eyes flitting over my face.

"Yes, you can. If he led a woman to believe they were engaged. Why did he get away with being a dirtbag, anyway?"

"He could be charming, as most con men are. People are fascinated by people who get away with pulling the wool over someone's eyes. Arthur did that better than most."

"Eek." The thought of someone getting away with conning anyone sickened me.

"In the corporate culture at Maxim's, you were considered more promotable with a woman at your side." He wandered to the family room and viewed the fireplace.

"It sounds like Arthur had several women."

"Let's just say he was exploring the field."

"Was he really engaged to be married?"

His shoulders straightened, and he pivoted toward me. His smile was lazy, but alert.

"That was a cover for upper management."

"So, no engagement?"

"He wouldn't say." Nate's handsome face was bland, but his twinkling eyes danced over my face. "I should go."

His cleft chin and mischievous twinkle distracted me, and I blurted, "I found a set of keys with the initials ABC engraved on them. They fit this house. You wouldn't know anything about them?"

"You should ask Penelope." He paused and gazed out of the picture window. "Penelope was elegant. Arthur would have been proud to have her on his arm."

"What about you?" I studied his firm chin and dimples.

He ran a hand through his hair and grinned, sheepish.

"I like women who are a little crazy."

"Excuse me?"

"Possessive." A smile flickered across his good looks.

"What?" I scrunched my face, amazed.

"My last girlfriend would follow me or wait in my car while I was at work."

"You're kidding! She was a stalker?"

He shrugged. "Some people might say that. It kept the relationship fresh and made me feel needed, special."

Speechless, I shook my head and stared at Nathan.

"Penelope and I could never be a match. She was refined, an immigrant in an awful marriage, but she had Sean and Arthur wrapped around her little finger. She didn't need me." He scoffed. "She could have her pick."

"So, you weren't attracted to her?" I asked, puzzled.

"She was beautiful, just not my type," he said.

Ah. The 'type.' I will never understand the mystery of attraction.

He drifted to the front door and turned toward me, his hand on the doorknob.

"Nice work. If I'm ever in need of a rehab specialist, I'll call." He gave me another careless grin, slipped on his sunglasses, and left.

Yikes. He was hot, so hot.

Chapter 37

Wayne arrived as Nathan motored out in his spiffy BMW. After watching him depart, I joined Wayne in the garage while he checked the mantel after the second coat of varnish.

"Who was that fella?" he nodded toward the convertible as it sped away.

"Nathan Winner. The other person of interest in the Maxim murder." I hadn't wanted to burden Wayne with my discoveries, but I needed to vent. "He said to ask Penelope about the keys I found." I mulled over his statement. "Penelope blocked my telephone number. What do you think Nathan means?"

"The keys could've been a gift." He looked at me quizzically.

"You think Penelope wanted to gift Arthur a set of keys?"

"Suppose she was going to give him keys to the house?" His mouth puckered. "She could have planned for Arthur to move in, so he could kick Sean out. With Arthur dead, plans change." Wayne could be pragmatic. It made him a good match for Gretta in her time of stress. He would stick by her through thick and thin.

"But it was Sean's house," I countered.

"Maybe it was symbolic. Your home is my home?" Wayne shrugged. "Or maybe he could sneak in without Sean's knowledge." He winked. That seemed more likely.

"So, Sean's story about how she didn't like his house was a lie? She threw the keys in a drawer and forgot about them?"

"Maybe he didn't know the keys were there. Sean wanted another house after Arthur's murder, more than she did. He wanted to get as far away as he could from the investigation."

"I suppose."

He gripped the mantel.

"Looks good," he said. "I'll take it inside." I followed him in and helped as he hoisted the new piece and put it in place.

"Great work. It will freshen up the place." I stood back and admired the simple slab.

"Thanks. It'll smell some. Might want to air out the place."

"Sure." I opened the family room windows, and then we went to the garage. He slipped a cigarette out of the pack in his front pocket and lit up. Leaning against the garage corner, he said, "It was quite a scene on Friday night," and sent me a sideways look, his brows raised.

"Yep. Enough said." I nodded.

"Glad Eddy was there," he said. "He scared off the dude."

"Me, too. Sean could have done a lot more damage." I cleared my throat and changed the subject from Sean's attempt to break in. "So, Gretta is sleeping better?" I winced; it wasn't working. "Probably not so much Friday."

"She's doing that whole sleep routine, a set bedtime, light meal, blackout drapes, cool room, no television, computer, phone, screens, etc., except for light snooze music."

"Good for her. How about you?" I was relieved to talk about another topic.

"Never did have problems sleeping." He grinned. "But I rest a lot easier with Gretta in bed all night."

"Good. I am going to do a run-through of the house before you secure the new mantel."

"I'll take Matilda for gas and get smokes." He winked.

"See you in a bit." I smiled, took my notepad, and walked through the house. Most items had been completed. I had touched up the paint from scuff marks. The kitchen was clean, cupboards and drawers empty. The new carpet needed vacuuming. I would leave that until I added some staging pieces for the showing and Wayne finished installing the mantel. I heard the creak of the overhead garage door, checked my watch, and frowned. Wayne had left the door open.

"Seems early for Wayne to be back." It had been barely ten minutes. I opened the connecting door to the garage and halted, frozen in place. Sean stood by the wall remote, one arm raised. The other hand gripped a mallet. We stood face to face. He scowled.

"Ack! What are you doing here?" His silent glare said nothing good. "Huh!" I inhaled, squeaked, slammed the door in his face, and locked it in a flurry of motion. Shaking, I dug for my phone in my pocket, and it slipped through my trembling fingers as he smashed the door casing with the weapon.

"You don't want to do this Sean!" I ran to the family room where Wayne had positioned the mantel, ready to install it.

"Says who?" He roared.

"Wayne's going to be back any minute!"

"I'll be gone, and you'll be dead! No one will ever know."

I thought of Dottie. "Your neighbor watches this house. She could be watching right now!" I danced away as he darted in with the mallet.

"You lie!" and he lunged again. I backed up, gripping the side of the wooden mantel.

"No, Sean. Be sensible. You do not want to get into any more trouble. They already suspect you of killing Arthur Cook and have eyewitness reports on you for battering my car and my house. Why, Sean?"

"Arthur was a pig! He had it coming! He was my enemy!" Sean shook with anger as he raised the mallet.

"That wasn't for you to decide," I said.

"I was home free until you started nosing around!"

"It was Penelope who asked Dottie to leave the bullet casing from the gun you used to shoot Arthur!" I countered, backing away, watching his hand with the weapon.

"No. She wouldn't!"

"Yes. Sean, she would, and she did. She connected you to his murder."

"It was the perfect murder, until you came along," he screamed. "He double-crossed me. He pretended he was my friend, but he was a mortal enemy! Arthur Cook conned everyone!"

"Not so perfect murder, when the police come to arrest you!" I felt for the side of the mantel that Wayne had crafted and steadied the weight. He raised the mallet, poised to strike.

"That pig was after my Penelope!"

"Penelope was going to leave you. Arthur was her way out of her miserable marriage to you!"

"He would not get my job AND MY WIFE! I would not let him!" He laughed maniacally; his eyes wide. I frowned and gripped the sides of the mantel.

"You should have seen his face when he sat in the cola." He leered. "And when I took his presentation, I watched him go through his desk, his briefcase, his coat pockets. We went out to lunch. He was an innocent. I faked being his friend and only meant to talk to him. But it got out of hand."

"Your wife was in love with him!"

"No! She was another one of his conquests. He said he had Penelope sewed up, along with my promotion. He was so smug. Then he mocked Arthur in a whiny voice, "He didn't want me to hear it from anyone else," he roared. "Then I knew he had to die!"

Grunting, he charged, his anger red hot, weapon held high. "I only had the gun for a short time. I tossed it in the river below the freeway by Maxim's." He brandished the mallet and gave another crazy laugh. Chills travelled my back. Sean was insane and a killer. He lunged.

"What, no gun now?" I yelled. I gripped the mantel. It was heavy and clumsy to wield, and it slipped in my grip. Sean saw his advantage and darted in to land a blow that glanced off the wood. I regained my hold and swung. The weapon clattered from his hand, and I rushed in with the thick wood, clunking him over the head. He dropped to his knees. His eyes glazed over, and he slumped to the floor.

Morgan Clark and another police officer charged in. She cuffed the man. "We heard the scuffle and yelling from the entry. Stuff him." Sean came to with a coughing spell. As he gagged, the officers brought him to his feet and marshaled him to the waiting squad car. "Read him his rights!"

A moment later, Don rushed in and came to my side, taking the mantel from my hands where I held it in a death grip.

"It is over now, Katelyn. You can relax." I heaved a sigh. Wayne peered around the door and asked, "You okay, Kiddo? I called the cops as soon as I saw that blue van in the driveway and the door was down."

"I've had better days. Your mantel saved my life."

Wayne took the wooden mantel from Don and examined it. "This is great lumber. Don't see a ding anywhere."

"Good job, Wayne," I said.

Don put his arms around me, and I smiled weakly.

"We'll take your account at the police station," Don said.

"All right. I will meet you there." He walked me to my SUV parked in the driveway and frowned. "I thought you said the car was fixed."

Gulping, "I said the windshield was repaired. The insurance covered that. Eddy did what he could."

"Eddy again?"

I shrugged and gave a wry smile.

"The car is ten years old. I dropped the collision thingy part of the coverage," I hedged and hit the key fob to open the doors. Don reached for the driver's door handle. The door didn't budge. I shook my head and went to the passenger's side. Opening the door, I climbed over the console to the wheel and waved. He closed his eyes and shook his head.

Chapter 38

It was late afternoon by the time all the chaos cooled down. After giving my report at the station, I finally arrived home. My mind had been on a nice, long soak in a bubble bath. Boots greeted me with a cool look.

"Don't you start," I warned him. He relented and wound his body around my legs, meowing, massaging my aching legs. "That's better." I filled his water and food dish, and he ate with gusto.

I filled the tub with the salt bath, lit the candle, and set a timer for 40 minutes to fully release any negativity. I slipped into the bath, reciting my intentions, "Return any bad juju to where it came from," and closed my eyes, feeling my body unwind. Hearing a key in the lock, I started and sat up. Throwing on a robe, I rushed from the bathroom.

"Dang it, Eddy, give me that key!" He halted, the house key in his hand.

"Oh, hey, Katie," he said. A smile stretched across his face, and his dark eyes sparkled. "Nice hair." I had put my hair in a towel while I soaked, and strands straggled out from under the wrap.

"Don't 'hey' me!" I held out my hand. "My key."

"I fixed your car," he reminded me, hurt, handing it over.

"Thanks Eddy. It looks better," I conceded. "No more coming in whenever you want."

"Okay." He nodded. "You won't be able to lower the driver's window. Thought you would want to know."

I hadn't tried the window, suspecting it wouldn't work with the dented door.

"Thanks. Good to know. Promise me? No more spare keys?"

"Yeah. All right," he was glum.

"Why aren't you at your place? With Lola?" I asked.

"She left."

"I'm sorry," I looked at him. "You're still working?"

"Yep," he said.

"So, it wasn't about not having a job."

"Not all of it," he admitted. The twinkle in his eyes dimmed.

"What, then?"

"She found someone else."

"Oh." I watched Eddy's shoulders slump. Now I felt like a heel. He must have had feelings for her if he was down.

"When did that happen?"

"The last time I lost my job, before the new job."

That explained why he kept dropping in at my place, at my renovation, and had fixed the car. Why he had been available. But he hadn't said anything.

"I'll put on the coffee and get dressed." Times like this required good, strong coffee or wine.

"Thanks, Katie." He headed to the sofa. Boots jumped up and perched on the edge behind his head and batted Eddy's hair as he sprawled out, groaning.

I hurried to the bathroom, noting that the timer had gone off, and I didn't know how many minutes I had been in the salt bath. Shrugging, I towel-dried my hair and ran a comb through the wet mass and left it to air dry. I headed to the bedroom and threw on jeans and a sweatshirt.

Eddy laid out on the sofa, his eyes shut, one hand holding his forehead as I passed him on the way to the coffeepot.

Pouring two mugs, I placed one on the coffee table in front of him and sat in the easy chair.

"You'll find someone else," I said. He sighed, sat up, and drank the brew.

"Yeah, I guess."

"You will." I didn't know why I should give Eddy a pep talk about finding another woman. He had done just fine while we were together. He was handsome and a charmer. After all, I had fallen for him once. I steeled myself against pity. We were both survivors, after all. Orphans had to be tough.

The strong java appeared to do its work, and he grinned. "Guess I thought I could make it work this time."

"Takes two." I sipped the Colombian brew.

"So, you're ready to take the big step. Huh, Katie?"

"This is about you." I blinked, my eyes wide.

"You look nervous." He looked through lowered lashes, a smile lingered.

"I won't lie, Eddy. I am scared."

"Sheriff's a good guy." He shrugged. "Promise you'll invite me to the wedding."

"Of course, Eddy. You're family." He grinned and finished his coffee with a flourish, placing the cup on the coffee table. The old Eddy was back. He stood, and we walked to the door. He threw his arms around me.

"Congratulations, Katie!"

I closed the door after him and asked Boots, who perched on the back of the sofa and watched me intently, "What just happened?"

He put his head between his paws and closed his eyes, ready to snooze.

Chapter 39

I listened to the weather report the next morning while I dressed for work. The announcer interrupted the broadcast with, "Last night, a man arrested for murder escaped from a local hospital where he was being treated for a head injury incurred during his arrest. His whereabouts are unknown. Be on alert. He is dangerous and may be armed." A clip from surveillance tape showed Sean Young walking past a vacant reception area and out of the hospital double doors. Gasping, I dialed Don.

"Sean Young escaped from the hospital?"

"Yes, he did."

"Why was he there?"

"He complained that his head hurt. We took him to the emergency room before we booked him. He was admitted."

"But how did he escape?" My mind ticked through the newscast. Nope, no info on how he had gotten away.

He paused.

"It is public knowledge. He waited until one officer went to the bathroom and the other fell asleep. He got the handcuff keys from the sleeping officer."

"Oh. My. God! Does he have a weapon?"

He hesitated, and I thought I would get the 'can't comment on an investigation,' routine, but he said, "We don't know."

"Great!" I exhaled.

"Both officers have their service weapons."

"But he could get a gun somewhere," I said.

"Yes. Be careful, Kate. I don't want you to get hurt."

"Me, either."

I had been blissfully unaware of the drama while I dealt with Eddy and unwound from the escapade of the day earlier. Now, my nerves were back on the brink of going into full-fledged panic.

"Steady girl," I muttered while I got my things together to head back to the renovation. It made little sense to lose another day's work for Sean Young. Logically, he wouldn't show up at the house he had just been arrested at. I stopped at Wayne's door.

"Think I'll stay in with Gretta, today. Lie low. I secured the mantel yesterday after the fracas. It's good to go," he said.

"No problem. Thanks Wayne."

"Be careful."

"I will. My bet is that he will go to his house in Minnetonka if he hasn't already fled to Canada."

"Could be right. Might be tough going anywhere wearing a hospital gown." He chuckled.

"He had a jacket, so that covered the nether regions." I snickered. "Must have stolen it from another room, or from the back of a chair. Better than an orange jumpsuit."

"Sure is." He sputtered and laughed.

I headed over to the renovation, stopping at the home store to buy new house numbers, a new mailbox, and a flat of pansies that would weather the cooler outdoor temperatures for my first showing, along with containers. My target date of April 1 was a week away, and I winced, banishing the thought that tricksters abound on April Fool's Day.

I sat in the driveway and admired the exterior. It was satisfying to see the brand spanking new garage door and see there wasn't any trace of a madman's attack. It was a dream that I could do what I love and get paid for it. Sure, there were some issues, but every job has challenges, I reminded myself. Look at Sean Young's dilemma. His coworker and fake friend got the promotion he wanted and snagged his wife in the process.

I climbed from the passenger's side of the SUV and got to work on the finishing touches. I unloaded the pansies into the garage and left the overhead door up and headed inside for a quick walk-through before I started potting the flowers for the home's curb appeal. It was when I came from the basement into the kitchen that I heard the garage door rumble. Pausing, I frowned and listened.

"Katelyn?" The woman's voice sounded high and nervous.

"Dottie?" My face scrunched, waiting, as I looked toward the garage entry door from inside the house.

"Yes. It's me." Her voice wavered, not the bubbly tone I was used to. She stumbled into the house, a man behind her, prompting her. My eyes widened in disbelief.

"Sean Young!"

"Don't do anything stupid," he said. "I have a gun. Dorothy is my hostage and my ticket out of this mess. If you make a move, she gets it in the back." His buzzed hair stood up, and his eyes were glazed over in desperation.

I held my hands up, trapped. If I moved, Dottie got shot. If I stood there, he could shoot me. The sleeve of the jacket shielded his hand. He wore skintight bright purple yoga pants and a tight black tee-shirt under the stolen jacket.

"Nice pants," I snarked. "Beats an orange jumpsuit."

He jabbed his hand in Dottie's back. She whimpered.

"Don't be funny." He scowled.

"They were the only clothes I could find for Mr. Young," Dottie said, trembling.

"Sorry, Dottie. Sean, what do you want?" I asked, keeping a close eye on the hand with the gun.

"I want new clothes, money, and a car."

"And I want to know how you did it, Sean?"

"I've got a gun!" he poked Dottie. She whimpered.

I gambled and said, "Sean, I have to sell this house. I do not want to tell a buyer someone was shot here."

"Then don't!"

"What happened to Arthur?"

"Took him for a long lunch and a short walk in a field," he spat, ending in a wild laugh, and I shuddered. "Shot him. No blood inside or near the van. I'm not stupid! Took the casings and stuffed them in the ashtray. They were my souvenirs," he whined. "Penelope found them and gave them to Dottie. Didn't she?" He pushed the gun into Dottie's back. She inhaled, her breath audible, shaking.

"Okay, that's all I wanted to know," I said soothingly. "I don't have any clothes here. I have about ten bucks in my purse. You're welcome to it. Let Dottie go. You do not want to add kidnapping to the charges you already have."

"Get your purse."

"Sure." My hands up, I walked toward my bag parked on the counter.

"No funny moves!" He jabbed the gun. Dottie's face paled. "Empty the contents on the floor where I can see them." I unloaded the messenger bag, which held an assortment of receipts, pens, a notepad, dusty chewing gum, and my wallet.

"Take out the money and credit cards. Write your bank card pin number down. Hurry!" I wrote the number on a piece of paper. *Good luck getting money out of that account.*

"Slide the stuff over here. I want your phone, too." I slipped the cell out of my pocket and slid the contents of my purse toward him. He went to one knee, watching me. The gun jabbed in Dottie's back. He scooped up the items with one hand and stuffed them in the pocket of his jacket. If Dottie had not been there, I would have taken my chances with rushing him. As it was, she looked as if she would faint.

"Give me your car keys!" I slid them over. "Now, walk to the bathroom."

"I don't have to go."

"I said, DON'T be funny." He scowled. "You follow her," he poked Dottie. We marched to the bathroom, my senses on overload. Was he going to shoot us in the bathroom? Made sense. Less cleanup. Smaller space.

Sean slammed the door behind us. We heard the doorknob being jammed by an object.

"Nobody moves for an hour!" We listened for his footfalls leaving the house, then I made for the door, rattling the knob.

"He braced it with something," I said. My mind ticked to the fold-up stepstool I used in the kitchen. "He must have used the stool to jam the knob." I looked around. "I'll go out the window."

"But he said to wait an hour. You could get shot." Dottie protested.

"If we wait, he'll get away. He might get to Penelope and kill her off, or anyone else who gets in his way." I unlatched the window, took off the screen, and cranked it open as wide as it could go. "You stay here."

She nodded, her eyes wide, mute with fear.

Standing on the toilet, I hoisted my body up, squeezed through the open window, and hit the ground. On the lawn, panicked, I needed an object, anything at all, for a weapon.

"Dottie, throw me the toilet brush!" I said, my voice hushed. She pitched it out the window, her face pinched and frightened. The brush was better than nothing. I gripped the handle and crept alongside the house. When I reached the driveway, Sean was struggling with the driver's door. Cursing, he went to the passenger's side. His derriere was on full purple display as he crawled over the console to the driver's wheel.

Three squad cars pulled up, one on either side of the car, with one blocking the rear. Surrounded, he panicked, ramming the car into reverse, hitting the car behind him. Trapped, he threw up his hands. Officers removed him from the car and took him away. It all happened so fast, and I waited, stunned. The sheriff's car pulled up, and Don jumped out and dashed to my side.

"Are you all right?" he asked.

"I'm okay. How did you get here so fast?"

"We were watching the house. When we saw Sean come out, we gave him enough time to wrestle with the car door and trap him inside."

"He had a gun. He could have shot someone."

"We didn't know if he had a gun, but thought it was doubtful. The gun he was after was gone. You found it and turned it over."

"And he knew that yesterday, when I hit him with the mantel. He used his finger to threaten Dottie." Recalling that his sleeve had covered his hand.

"Yep."

"So, why come here?"

"Closer to the hospital. He knew Dottie, and he could get clothes, money, and anything else he needed for a getaway. He saw an opportunity to take two people, you and Dottie, as hostages."

"But he took my money, credit cards, and car instead."

"He likely thought hostages would slow him down. He wanted a fast getaway."

"Hellooooo! Is anyone there?" It was Dottie yelling from the bathroom window.

"We should get her out," I said.

We went into the house, and sure enough, it had been my stepstool that jammed the doorknob. Dottie's eyes were huge, and she babbled, "He's gone, right? He showed up this morning while I sat outside watching the birds, and suddenly, he was on my deck with a gun! Then he wanted clothes, and I didn't have anything that fit except those yoga pants, and very little money, and my car was in the shop. It was a nightmare." She took a deep breath. "Anyway, it was about that time Katelyn showed up and he forced me over here. You know, I have a bad heart." She clutched her chest. "I can't take a lot of stress. It was bad enough when he lived here, but this is beyond reason. No wonder Penelope wanted out!" She gasped again, breathing heavy.

"It's over, Dorothy," Don said.

"You're sure? It was supposed to be over yesterday." Dottie's voice rose.

"As sure as we can be," Don said. "He's in custody."

"Ack. I'm going home." She turned and left out the front door, muttering, "He was in custody when he escaped!"

"She's right, you know," I said.

"Who was guarding him at the hospital?"

Don's face flushed. "It'll be in the news," he admitted. "It was a new hire and Morgan Clark."

"Morgan went to the bathroom, and the newbie fell asleep," I guessed.

"Appears so." Don cleared his throat. "Could have happened to anyone."

"What happens to them?"

"The newbie is no longer an employee. Morgan is suspended, pending an investigation."

"Well, then. I am going home now. I have a bathtub and a nice long soak waiting for me."

"Your car is toast."

"Can I get a ride?" I asked, and batted my lashes.

"Sure." He grinned. We walked to the sheriff's car. My car was hooked to a tow truck, being impounded as we left. The back was crunched, and I wondered aloud if it would start.

"Doesn't matter," Don said. "It is part of an investigation now. It was used in a commission of a crime, crashing a police car. You probably won't get it back, and if you do, you will not want it."

"Bummer," I said, sat back and closed my eyes. "I guess that's going to be part of the renovation cost." He left me at the townhouse with a kiss and a promise to be back.

"Not tonight. I think I would like some 'alone' time."

"Sure." He held me close. "Call me when you want to talk."

"Uh, huh." I did not want to talk to anyone about anything.

This time, I vowed I would take the full recommended time for a salt bath to remove any bad energy that was attached to me. I ran the tub water and put in earplugs to drown out anyone at the door. I took the house phone off the receiver and turned off my cellphone. Setting the timer, I sank into the sudsy water and closed my eyes, unwinding, considering my intentions. While I meditated, Boots wandered in and out of the bathroom.

    The timer went off after the required time was up. I was satisfied. Now the bad juju was banished and tomorrow would be a whole new game.

Chapter 40

"Hey Kiddo," Wayne knocked at my door early the next morning. "Heard there was some excitement at the rehab yesterday."

"Sean Young escaped and was captured at the renovation." I waved him in.

"Sorry I missed it," he said.

"No worries."

"Do you need me for anything today?"

"Well, I could use a ride. Sean rammed my car, and the police department has taken it. I have new house numbers and a mailbox to install."

"I'll get Matilda out and meet you out front."

"Sounds good."

While Wayne installed the new mailbox, I nailed new house numbers on the home. At least I could tell any potential homebuyer that the house had not had a murder. I felt satisfied as I went through the final cleanup. Sean was in custody, for good this time (fingers crossed), and he had confessed to killing Arthur where his body had been found.

I was putting out the 'For Sale' sign as Don drove up in his steady Buick. Close behind was Morgan Clark, driving the official sheriff's car. He got out, while Morgan traded the driver's side for the passenger's side in the sheriff's vehicle.

"Hey, Kate. You feel better today?"

"Downright chipper," I said, beaming. "Morgan's off suspension, I see?"

"Yep. Internal affairs cleared her of any wrongdoing."

"That was fast," I said.

"Yes. They can work fast if they want." He grinned.

"Good. And Sean is still in custody?"

"Yes. I want you to drive the Buick until we get you a new car."

"The Ford is pretty much totaled." I frowned.

"Yes. Can't have my future wife driving a wreck." He smiled and handed me the keys. "I have an image to protect."

I raised my brows. "Image, you say?"

"Let me correct that." He put his arms around me, and said, "I have a woman I care dearly about, that I want driving a safe vehicle. The Buick is very safe."

"Better." I wrinkled my nose. "Morgan is watching us, you know."

He chuckled and leaned over to kiss my forehead. "Let her."

"Hello!" Dottie called from next door, startling us. We dropped our embrace and watched her stout figure trek across the lawn. "So, I will get an invitation to the wedding, won't I? It's mandatory when a neighbor is taken hostage during a manhunt."

"Sure, Dottie, you are on the invitation list." I smiled.

"Can I bring a guest?"

"Of course."

"Good." She caught her breath. "I'll bring Penelope. It has been rough on her seeing her husband arrested for murder, escape, then captured again. Poor woman just wants to have a normal life, be done with Sean Young. This will give her an outing to look forward to. It's a shame you're selling now. We were just getting to know one another during that whole hostage taking thing and everything." My eyes glazed over, and Don discreetly looked over at Morgan, watching from the passenger's side, window down, smirking while Dottie talked.

"Gotta go," Don whispered. "Call you later." He edged away while Dottie continued to talk. He waved as he drove away with Morgan.

My eyes wide and glassy, Wayne winked at seeing my discomfort and joined us while Dottie followed at my heels. I placed the basket of pansies in front of the door under the new house numbers.

"Pansies are great. Anybody who buys this house will love what you have done. It looks so much fresher, and a young family will lov . . .."

"Thanks, Dottie. I have a few more things to do inside." I smiled. Wayne was behind me as we entered and closed the door.

"Oh, okay, I'll get going." We peeked out the window and breathed a sigh as she retreated.

"She's a talker, all right," Wayne said.

"You think?" I laughed.

"So, I guess you won't need a ride home now?"

"No, you can take off."

"Great, promised Gretta we'd go to the nursery for spring flowers and out to eat."

"Go for it. I want to look around, see if there is anything I missed."

Satisfied after I made another walk through, I locked up the house, straightened the 'For Sale' sign, and drove away in the cushy Buick. The seat felt like a deep sofa, with a smooth, almost surreal quiet ride.

Don called later and offered to take us out in his jazzy Corvette. My nerves were soothed by driving the Buick. "Let's stay in at your house. I will pack up Boots and see you later."

"Great idea."

***

After dinner, we relaxed in the great room. We had a wedding planning session, in which he agreed small is better. A few close friends and family in Myra's backyard, who had graciously offered her home.

"We need to talk about Morgan," Don said.

"So, talk." Morgan Clark had been a minor thorn in my side. She had not given my calls to Don, and she spent a fair number of late nights with him. His explanation had been that they were catching up on paperwork. Morgan was a zealot for writing tickets, good for Crocus Heights revenue, but a drain on the department resources.

"I have been training Morgan to take over as sheriff. I will support her in the election. When my term is up, I am stepping down." His four-year term was ending soon. "I've been kicking it around for a while."

"Okay." Now, I got it. Those late work nights meant he had been training her to possibly run for Sheriff. "Then what?" I liked Morgan more. I would worry less about Don's safety if he wasn't serving the public.

"I'll take some time getting used to being a civilian, being married." He grinned. "I could start a detective agency." Well, maybe he'd be in a safer job.

"Really?" Then the idea excited me. "We could catch the bad guys together. Wouldn't that be fun? Like Sherlock Holmes and Watson, wouldn't that be an adventure?"

"I thought you enjoyed being a home rehab specialist. That you didn't want to give it up?"

"I have solved so many mysteries in the houses I've done. It could be a side gig."

"Uh, huh. Private detective work can be boring. We would need some time apart."

"Boring? How?"

"It can be a lot of work doing investigations. Long stretches where nothing much happens."

"Exactly why it could be a side gig."

"Sometimes terrible domestic situations."

"Like Sean and Penelope." I was circumspect.

"Yes."

"So, do you know what happened to Penelope?"

"After Sean went to jail, she filed for divorce. After that, it is anyone's guess."

"Dottie would know. She kept in touch with her."

"True. It was not the smartest thing for her to leave that bullet casing, even if it was for a good friend."

"Is she in any trouble?"

"Until Sean Young is prosecuted, the investigation is open."

Chapter 41

It was an all but done deal with a young couple with two children, a boy, and a girl. I was plastering a 'Sold' sticker across the sale sign as they were getting in their Dodge Caravan. Dottie traipsed across the lawn, and she yelled a cheery 'hello' to the couple who were about to drive away.

The woman rolled down her passenger's side window and greeted the neighbor.

"Did you just buy the house?" Dottie asked, puffing, out of breath.

"Yes, we signed the papers. We can't wait to move in."

"You know about the almost murder here?" she asked.

The woman, a redhead, went paler than her normal shade of creamy white. Her husband, with deep chestnut brown hair, sighed. The kids, the girl about eight and the boy about ten, were in the back seat.

"Cool!" the boy's face lit up. His hair was the same color as his mother's, and his complexion full of freckles.

"We were going to wait to tell the kids about the disturbance. But nothing happened in the house? Right?" the woman asked.

"Not unless you call an escaped criminal hiding out, nothing." She chortled.

"Wow! Super cool." The young boy snickered. "An escaped convict hid out here?"

"This is Dorothy Barker, your next-door neighbor," I introduced her. "Dottie, I thought I saw the mailman earlier?"

"Oh, I'd better check the mail. Great to see a young couple with kids move in. That house was a disaster with that last couple. Not so much his wife, but Sean Young was a real problem."

"Dottie?" I bit my bottom lip. "Thank you for stopping."

"Sure." She headed to the mailbox.

I braced myself, waiting for the deal to go south. I had disclosed about the prior owner, but had sanitized the account, saying there had been unfortunate dealings with the prior owner's arrest, but nothing lethal. Which was technically true.

"We looked up the prior owners of the house in the tax records, and found the newspaper accounts," the redhead said.

"We don't have a problem," the husband added. He chuckled. "It adds to the kids' excitement about getting a bigger house."

"Great," I grinned. "It has a story."

"Yeah! Pretty cool, huh?" the boy chimed.

"I think it's neat, too," said the girl who had been quiet until then. "A real criminal!"

"Glad to hear it," I said. They took off. *Wow, that was a close call.*

***

After the house closed, Don and I celebrated with a dinner at Joseph's.

"I want to show you a place that could work for us," he said.

"Awesome!" I was jazzed he'd been out scouting for our together home.

He parked in front of a lot on Hidden Lake with a 'For Sale' sign and a builder's name on the signage. We got out of the car.

"How about we build *our* home here?"

I gazed at the lake and back at the forested lot. From out of the dense woods, seven deer tripped across the lot, startled, the white underside of their tails twitched, and they ran toward the lake. We watched the deer, transfixed.

"It's perfect," I said.

"We won't be able to complete the home until after the wedding?"

"It'll be perfect."

"So, you and Boots are good with living at my home until the house is built?"

"Yep."

"Then it's settled. We'll move you the week before the wedding."

I hesitated, my gut seized, and then relaxed.

"But I want to see house plans and the lot cleared for our home," I said.

"We can start tonight." Wrapped in each other's arms, we talked and watched the ripples on the lake until the moon rose and the stars came out.

Chapter 42

Two months later.

The day of the wedding came, and we gathered in Myra's backyard for the small ceremony in mid-June. The topiary was nicely groomed, and the day was sunny. She was my maid of honor. Our shopping adventure netted a simple tea length off-white dress, and I carried a bouquet of red roses. Her stylist groomed my hair, and it was perfect. She wore a lovely light green dress that brought out the flecks of green in her hazel eyes. She placed her arm around my waist when I felt a panic attack threaten.

Don beamed as we stood under an arched trellis filled with garland against the backdrop of the 'couples' lake where we said our vows. He was dashing in formal wear, the flecks of silver in his blond hair caught by the afternoon sun. His cobalt blues were sure and steady. Esther cared for Boots, who wore a bow tie for the occasion, and which went well with his tuxedo coat. He was on a leash, satisfied with a catnip mouse and a cheerful attendant in Esther.

After much back and forth, Don and I agreed that Bernie, who performed Wayne's and Gretta's ceremony, would be a fitting choice for the officiator. That was when Don originally proposed, but I debated whether he was serious.

Bernie, in a high tenor voice and wild hair, pronounced us husband and wife, and we kissed. As we embraced, his boom box was queued to play Michael McDonald's "(Your Love Keeps Lifting Me) Higher and

Higher." Everyone cheered and boogied to the beat of the music as we proceeded to the dining room where the reception dinner was held. The banquet size table held enough seats for the intimate wedding, and we ate a marvelous catered dinner of prime rib, mashed potatoes, and all the trimmings.

Eddy, looking sheepish, came solo, and zoomed in on Penelope, who appeared very elegant, and who came with Dottie, as she promised. He took each woman's arms and escorted them to the table. Gretta and Wayne came. She had done her hair in a striking pink and wore a lilac-colored summer dress. Wayne had done his gray hair in a braid that flowed down his back and wore a linen vest over a purple shirt with linen pants. Myra's companion, Charlie the electrician, was a portly, brown-haired, jovial man who squeezed her hand at the dining table. We ordered the cake from the Pastry Palace, who also made wedding cakes. After toasts, Charlie entertained the party with corny electrician jokes during the dinner.

"What's an electrician's favorite band? AC/DC" he answered.

Everyone groaned, laughed good-naturedly, drank champagne, and feasted on the scrumptious meal.

Dottie talked incessantly to Eddy while he maintained an admiring side-eye on Penelope, who kept her eyes averted.

After dinner, I excused myself to the restroom. Myra had offered the use of her owner's suite during the big day. I climbed the grand staircase to the en suite.

"Excuse me!" I said, nearly running into Dottie as she left the bathroom. Her handbag was open, and we were both startled. She hastily closed her purse. I blinked. "Is that the silver in your purse, Dottie?"

"Don't be silly." She gave a little giggle and started toward the door.

"Stop," I grabbed her arm. "Dottie, open your purse!"

Her face turned bright red, and she slowly opened the bag. I lifted out a set of silver and a pair of diamond stud earrings.

"Is this everything?" Her face red, mutely, she nodded. "Nothing in your pockets?"

She shook her head, no.

I sifted through the handbag, and satisfied, said, "You have to leave now." I took her arm and led her down the staircase and out the front door to her car, while the rest of the guests gathered in front of the lake, under a canopy set up for the day. "Does Penelope know what you do?" I demanded.

She shook her head, still mute, her head down.

"Go, now." My arms folded across my chest; I watched her drive away.

"Is everything okay?" Don asked, coming up behind me.

"We will chat later," I said soberly. "Dottie had to leave."

Baffled, he said, "All right, we can talk then." A slight frown creased his face.

"I have to use the bathroom," I said, and kissed him quickly. "And then I have to talk to Myra." My mind raced. What on earth could I say to her? I trusted Dottie, and now everything she had done or said was an open question. Was Penelope part of a ruse? Had she asked Dottie to plant the casing to divert from her part in Arthur's murder? Had Dottie played a part in the murder?

On second thought, I asked. "You're still the sheriff, right?"

"Good grief, Katelyn. What is it?"

I told him about Dottie's actions and asked, "Was Penelope's whereabouts confirmed for the time when Arthur was murdered?"

"Yes. She was at her mother's."

"Her mother was her alibi?" I arched my brow.

"She had gas receipts and yes, her mom verified her visit."

"Okay," I said.

"Hey, where'd Penelope go?" Eddy asked, looking dismayed. He ran his hands through tousled hair and loosened his tie.

"Dottie must have called her," I said. Don nodded.

"I'll call Morgan." He winked and went outside to the Buick, where he had left his cellphone.

"What's going on?" Eddy looked at me.

"He's just making a quick call. He'll be right back," I said.

"You're a beautiful bride again." He grinned. "Great party. Congratulations!"

"Thanks Eddy." He threw his arms around me in a hug.

Don returned, and we held hands and went back to our guests, finishing the night with more champagne toasts.

I hadn't had the heart to tell Myra someone I brought into her home was a petty thief. I put her earrings back in the jewelry case on her dresser and brought the silver to the kitchen. She was thrilled with the wedding, and Charlie made her smile. Little did she know how memorable the day was.

***

We spent the week before we left on our honeymoon relaxing at Don's mansion. I was becoming more and more at home in his place and Boots was adapting too. I overheard him speaking with Morgan and couldn't contain my curiosity.

"What happened with Penelope?" I asked.

"Morgan interrogated her again. Penelope spent the weekend of Arthur's murder at her mother's and could account for all their time spent together. Penelope admitted she asked Dottie to hide the bullet casing in the garage. She found the casings in the van, and put two and two together with Arthur's murder, and felt trapped. Although she was despondent over his death, she had heard the rumors about other women. She was angry at Arthur, but more scared of what Sean was capable of."

"So, she was trying to help the police in their investigation."

"Yes."

"Why not just go to the police?" I asked.

"As an immigrant, she was afraid they wouldn't believe her. If they didn't and Sean found out, it could have been very bad for her."

"What about Dottie planting evidence?"

She sincerely wanted to help a friend in a bad domestic situation. She is harmless. But Dottie has sticky fingers. The new owners will have to monitor her."

"Or she'll watch them." I chuckled.

Chapter 43

Don insisted on making all the arrangements for our honeymoon. I was good with that if it didn't involve a classic Corvette ride. He chartered a private plane, and we flew to Hawaii. From the white recliners to the wide aisles on the private charter, it was breathtaking.

"This must have cost a fortune," I murmured as we boarded.

"Yep." He agreed. "And worth every penny." He held my hand and brushed the hair off my forehead. We sank into cushy seats and gazed at the ground beneath us as the plane took off.

A few minutes later, I closed the shade, my stomach queasy as the buildings below looked like matchbooks the higher we got.

"Champagne?" he asked. The flight attendant placed an ice bucket with a bottle on the table in front of us.

"Please." He popped the cork and poured us each a glass.

"To our new life," he said, and we tapped our flutes.

The champagne went down effortlessly, and I held out my glass. "More, please." After we finished the bottle, while the plane flew smoothly to the island, I closed my eyes. Unwinding for the first time in months as the impact of our vows set in, I fell asleep and woke when we landed.

Whisked away in a limo, the driver pulled up in front of a luxury hotel.

"Not sure I have the wardrobe for this." Inhaling, I stepped from the luxury car while the bellhop loaded our luggage. I gazed at the palm trees and smelled the scent of tropical flowers. "This is beautiful." I gazed at Don. "How much money did you say you have?"

"Enough for a great honeymoon." He grinned. "And more."

Squee!

The End

Katelyn's Home Improvement Tips

- Moving with a pet is stressful for the pet and human alike. A tee shirt or something with your scent placed in their new area will calm the creature.
- Provide hiding places for a cat while they get used to a new environment, a box, their crate, paper bags. A cat tower in front of a window provides shelter with a view.
- If possible, a window seat for canine or feline pets provides a restful and/or entertaining spot.
- Provide a small rug or a carpet sample for kitty to scratch on, dispose of when shredded.
- Keep washable fabrics in mind for furniture or keep a throw handy to cover furniture if pets have free range inside.
- Try to maintain a routine for pets as much as possible while transitioning to a new house.
- Keep a radio on with soft music to calm the pet while you are away.
- It may take a few months for your furry companion to become comfortable in a new place.
- Keep a bin in a cupboard, console, or under an end table to collect kitty or dog toys.
- There are new gadgets for cat litter that are like a piece of furniture, and more appealing to pet owners.
- Check with your vet for possible calming medications if traveling long distances with your pet, on a plane or in a car.
- Be patient with your pet and kind to yourself while making big changes.

Acknowledgements

Many people deserve my gratitude for their support, friendship, and work associated with the Home Renovator Series, including libraries and bookstores. My sincere thank you to the following:

Thank you to Betty Borns, for our many years of friendship, fun and encouragement in this journey. Joe Sebesta and Judith Anne Horner, beta readers; Dr. Jen Prosser, for her expertise on poisons, https://www.pickpoison.com/; Twin Cities Sisters in Crime; Guppies; the Word Whippers Critique Group: William Anderson, Cathlene Buchholtz, Dale Butler, Barb Danson, and Mary Rodgers for their continuing support. And a grateful thank you to my readers.

About the Author

M.E. Bakos writes cozy mysteries about a house flipper, turned sleuth, in fictional Crocus Heights, Minnesota. The series has earned five-star reviews from Readers Favorite. Her mystery short stories receive kudos. She has published short stories in Twin Cities Sisters In Crime anthologies and was a regular fiction contributor to national women's magazines.

If she isn't plotting mysteries, she's planning home improvements. She lives in Minnesota with her husband, Joe Sebesta, and a spoiled pooch named Chipper.

Also By, and Contact Information:

You can reach her at: mebakos@yahoo.com
On Facebook: https://www.facebook.com/mebakos/
https://www.facebook.com/mary.sebesta.90/
Website: https://mebakos.wixsite.com/author
Read the Series:
Fatal Flip, Book 1
Deadly Flip, Book 2
Lethal Flip, Book 3
Killer Flip, Book 4.
All have five-star ratings from Reader's Favorite.

www.ingramcontent.com/pod-product-compliance
Lightning Source LLC
LaVergne TN
LVHW041918070526
838199LV00051BA/2658